WILD IRISH GRACE

THE MYSTIC COVE SERIES, BOOK 7

TRICIA O'MALLEY

LOVEWRITE PUBLISHING

WILD IRISH GRACE

The Mystic Cove Series

Copyright © 2018 by Lovewrite Publishing
All Rights Reserved

Cover Design:
Alchemy Book Covers
Editor:
Elayne Morgan

If you would like to do any of the above, please seek permission first by
contacting the author at:
info@triciaomalley.com

Dedicated to the difficult women in this world. May we hear you roar.

"Well-behaved women seldom make history." ~ Laurel Thatcher Ulrich

CHAPTER 1

*H*e'd come to her once again, in her dreams, as he had since she'd come of age. A man she'd loved across centuries, for lifetimes, and yet had known so very little of in real life. Her love for him was like a star, each evening searing her soul with its heat, night upon night, until she could only hope that one day the star would collapse in on itself, leaving her dreams finally free of the one man she measured all others against.

Dillon Keagan.

Frustrated, and very aware of needs unmet, Grace sighed and pulled a pillow over her head, running a small spell in her mind to charm herself free of the dreams. They had increased of late and had robbed her of any peaceful moments of sleep over the past several months.

Her power carried her only so far, drifting softly in the grey in-between of awake and dreaming. Then, once more, she found herself walking on the shore, irresistibly drawn to the man who laughed to her from where he stood knee-deep in water, a fishing line in hand, the ocean breezes kissing his curls.

"I've a mighty feast for us this evening, Gráinne, that I do," Dillon called to her as he added another fish to the almost-full basket that lay wedged between two rocks on the shore. Grace smiled at him, battling a shyness so unnatural to her that she wanted to overcompensate by coming up with a bawdy joke to tell him. Instead she caught her toe on a rock and let out a stream of curses usually reserved for sailors as she hopped on one foot, her cheeks flaming in embarrassment.

"You've a mouth on you, that you do, my pretty Gráinne," Dillon laughed, coming to her and sweeping her up in his arms, dazzling her with his charm and the way his eyes crinkled at the corners when he laughed. Blue as the sea when the first rays of sun streamed across its surface in the morning, Dillon's eyes captivated her with their warmth, laughter, and how they spoke of worlds unknown.

Grace wanted to know those worlds, to hear him tell tales of cities both near and far, and to know who this man was and how'd he'd come to land on her shores. Shores she guarded fiercely and had made a name for herself in ruthlessly protecting.

Oh, but she never wanted to leave this place, Grace thought as she nuzzled into his neck, allowing him to carry her like a helpless maiden to the abandoned hut they'd commandeered, where they had spent the last few weeks hopelessly lost in each other's arms. Dillon had been as much of a surprise to her as she to him: he a shipwrecked sailor clinging to the tatters of his boat, and she – an unexpected woman captain of a sleek little sloop – his rescuer. She'd spared him her usual treatment of the vagabonds she'd discovered on the water, whether it was because of his striking good looks – sun-kissed curls and dancing blue eyes – or the fact that she'd known since the moment she'd laid eyes upon him that their lives were somehow inextricably connected.

Grace had docked near a small village on the west coast and sent her crew on home to their families. There had been too many battles and her men were weary. A good leader knew when her crew was spent, and it had been months since many of them had slept in a bed or known the warm arms of a lover. They'd return in a month's time, replenished and refueled, and ready for whatever battle they'd next need to fight.

But for now, in this moment, this part of the world was hers and Dillon's alone. It was their own little island of discovery and exploration, and they dove into it with delight, exchanging stories of battles both won and lost, and sights seen across the seas.

They made love with abandon, late into the night, while the fire burned low and their bodies burned hot, each touch an exploration, an awakening. When Grace looked into his eyes, the edges of her world and his blended to become one.

It felt like coming home.

After hours spent exploring each other, she lay liquid and supple, her eyes on the light that just creased the horizon of the water. The fire was long dead and Grace shivered.

"What worries you, my love?" Dillon's voice, sleepy

and sated at her ear, sent warm tendrils down her neck as he pulled her back close to his chest, his body cradling hers in warmth.

"I can't stay here – in this moment with you. I have children who need me, tenants who depend on my lead since my husband has passed, boundaries to defend, and treasures to preserve. How am I to stay here – tucked away in this hut – forever?" Grace said, her eyes heavy with sleep and something more, an ache of knowing that this moment of pure joy was not to be forever.

She'd had many highs and lows in her short but fiercely-lived life, and a realist she was – Gráinne O'Malley, the great pirate queen of the Irish seas. But buried deep beneath her warrior's shell was a fiercely romantic heart that cherished love in all its forms. It was both her greatest strength and biggest weakness. Her gaze landed on the stone they'd engraved together, branding the cottage as their own.

My heart for yours.

Dillon turned her so that she met his eyes, the sun's light just enough so that they shone intensely blue in his face as he gazed down on her, his look both a caress and a promise. Raising her hand to his lips, he first kissed it before bringing both their hands to her heart.

"You'll have this moment, forever, here in your heart. Once a love like ours is known, it can never be taken from us, and transcends all barriers – those of mortal law, those of time, and beyond what most can comprehend. It's an endless love, one that grows through the ages, and we'll meet, time and time again, our souls knowing each other, our love binding us for centuries. Be it but weeks of time in this life, know that we're promised for more, Gráinne O'Malley, for it is written in the tapestry of the universe."

Grace lost herself in his words. She'd heard them time and again in her dreams, and yet each time he uttered his promises of a love that knew no boundaries she was sucked back in, the pain of love and loss a bittersweet taste in her mouth.

Sighing, Grace pulled the pillow from her head and sat up in bed, annoyed with herself for wanting both to weep in longing and to laugh for the sheer joy of having felt such a love fill her soul. Granted, it was only in her dreams – dreams where she walked as Gráinne O'Malley and not as herself, Grace O'Brien, in the now – but to know that such a love existed was like being in the desert and seeing the hint of water on the horizon.

Try as she might, Grace had never found out what happened to Dillon or how he and Gráinne had parted ways. Though she had many gifts of magick, remembering all the bits of her past lives was not one of them. Some historical records reported that Dillon was a shipwrecked sailor Grace had taken as a lover before he'd been murdered on Donegal land. Gráinne had spent her life avenging his murder, even after she'd taken a new husband; she'd never forgiven the Donegal clan and had gone on to seize their castle and make them regret the day they'd ever wronged Gráinne O'Malley. A part of Grace hoped the story was true, for she was known to have a fiercely vengeful side that rarely forgave a grievous slight, but the part where Dillon was murdered made Grace hope that the threads of time had come unwoven and a happier ending had come to her love.

Grace tugged her hair and ran her hands over her face, taking a few deep breaths to calm herself. In the past few months the lines between the worlds had begun to shift and blur even more than was natural for her, an exceptionally powerful healer and practitioner of all things magick. With this shift in energy, Dillon had begun visiting her in her dreams nightly, causing her to ache each morning as though she'd lost the love of her life once more.

It was a decidedly uncomfortable way to wake up.

"Enough of that nonsense," Grace said to Rosie, granddaughter of Ronan the Great, who wagged her tail at the foot of the bed, her eyes alight with excitement over her impending breakfast.

"Come on, Rosie, let's have ourselves a day off. We haven't had a day of fun in a while," Grace decided, and the dog did a spin of joy at the end of the bed. Looking at her iPhone, Grace reminded herself of the date and what year she lived in.

For though she'd once walked the shores as Gráinne O'Malley, her soul lived in the here and now, and she would do well to remember that. Lover or no, Grace had a life to live and a destiny to fulfill.

CHAPTER 2

*G*race didn't entirely know what a day off looked like, for when work was both a love and a passion, they blended seamlessly together. She rarely put boundaries up between the two. Why bother? Work filled her with great joy and a sense of purpose – plus it tied her to the gifts of her bloodline, handed from Fiona to Keelin and on to her.

Healing wasn't her only gift, not by far, but it was the most rewarding one, Grace thought as she tilted her head and poured an extra bit of lavender into a pain-relief cream she was working on for Mrs. Donan's arthritis. It had been damp weather of late and she knew the old woman was struggling. With a glance at the stormy clouds that held a promise of rain on the horizon, Grace decided that staying in for the day had been a good choice.

"We'll have us a lovely catch-up day with our supplies, won't we, Rosie? I'll put on some music and stoke the fire – we can even have a dance party," Grace said, beaming down at the pup who was her virtual shadow. Idly braiding her sunset-colored hair and tucking it over her shoulder, Grace hummed her way across the room to stoke the peat in the small stove that sat nestled in front of a beautiful wooden rocking chair. The chair – hand-carved, its edges now worn smooth by love – had been a gift from John to his Fiona on their wedding day, along with the cottage that Grace now lived in.

Losing Fiona three years ago had been a blow to her entire family – in fact, all of Grace's Cove had mourned her passing. But at a hundred and three years of age, Fiona had finally decided enough was enough and had passed easily into the next realm. Her passing had barely fazed Grace – another gift of hers that she sometimes considered to be both a blessing and an annoyance.

"You've had another one of your dreams, haven't you?"

"Haven't I told you it's rude to be popping into a person's living room uninvited, old woman?" Grace complained, glancing over her shoulder to where Fiona sat at the kitchen table, looking as human as ever, surveying with a critical eye the various supplies and ingredients laid out in front of her.

"You'll be remembering it was my cottage first," Fiona said, her nose in the air, but a twinkle in her eye took the sting from her words. Sure and it had been a shock to Grace when she'd walked into Fiona's cottage the day after the funeral to begin sorting through Fiona's stuff and had found the old woman relaxing in her rocking chair as if nothing unusual had come to pass. It wasn't the first time Grace had seen a ghost, but it was certainly her longest and most involved interaction with one. Having

Fiona near had brought great comfort to Grace and her family, and even though she'd taken on the role as a translator of sorts for her family, she quickly found that they could all still communicate with Fiona in their own ways.

Hers was just the most direct.

"How could I forget? You still live here," Grace grumbled.

Fiona laughed, knowing that Grace loved having her around. "You've a need for me yet," she said, her eyes knowing as she continued to catalog the contents of the kitchen table that had once been hers. It had served thousands of meals and hundreds of visitors through the years.

"Of course I do," Grace said, moving to the stove where her teapot had begun to sing. "Your wisdom transcends all time. Though you're welcome to go visit the others, you know. You don't always have to hang out here." Grace feigned grumpiness while she poured her tea, knowing that Fiona enjoyed their banter.

"My other chicks are well sorted. It's you I've got my eye on," Fiona said, tilting her head to study the shadows under Grace's eyes. "You've lost a bit of weight."

"And I've more that I could lose. A slender build is not in my bloodline," Grace said, adding sugar and milk to her tea. Being voluptuous didn't bother Grace overmuch; in olden days it had been a sign of wealth and prestige – signifying that she was prosperous enough to feed herself and her family. It was only in this world that it seemed everyone was so involved in looking perfect, paying so much attention to a number on the scale, that they forgot to just live their lives. Grace knew how fleeting a lifetime could be. Wasting that time fussing over whether her bum looked good in a skirt was useless. If one man didn't find it appealing, another would – or so she reminded herself with a sigh as she settled at the table. Her dating life had been virtually nonexistent in the past year, and not for lack of interest.

"You don't need to lose weight and you know that. Now, tell me, was it the same dream?" Fiona asked, her gaze shrewd as she studied her granddaughter's face.

"It was, once again. And…" Grace was shocked to hear her voice catch, and she rushed to sip her tea, which she immediately regretted when it scalded her tongue. Choking, she shook her head for a moment and held up a finger for Fiona to wait while she swallowed and ran some quick magick to deal with her pain. Once she was sorted, she met Fiona's eyes. "And… I wake up feeling like I've lost the love of my life. Over and over. It's exhausting. I don't know what I'm meant to do or how to rid myself of these dreams."

"Maybe you're not meant to rid yourself of them," Fiona said.

"But I can't keep living like this. How can I grieve the loss of a lover I've never had? Never known? At least not in this lifetime."

"Have you asked him for a message? In your dream?" Fiona asked. "Maybe he's trying to communicate something."

"I… no, I haven't," Grace admitted, tucking one foot beneath her and absently rubbing Rosie's ear, who had come to sit by her at the table, resting her head on Grace's leg. "I get so swept up in reliving those moments on the shore that I'm just *there*, you know? I know it's me and it's not me at the same time, but I feel it so deeply that I forget I can guide or ask for things in my dream. Lucid dreaming... I just... it's like the dam breaks on my emotions and all I can do is feel, not think, and I'm both the happiest and the saddest I've ever been in one night."

"That does sound exhausting," Fiona said, leaning back a bit as she studied her great granddaughter. "Living with loss is incredibly difficult."

"You lived it. With losing John so young. How did it not break you?" Grace asked, propping her head on her hand as she toyed with a scone she'd put on a plate in front of her.

"I had Margaret to worry about. As an empath, she was basically a sponge for my emotions. My anguish was killing her. I taught myself to lock it away and to only bring it out in small moments – down in the cove – or when one of the family would take her away. It was a lesson in strength and compartmentalizing."

"See? That's amazing to me. I admire you so much for the hardships you dealt with in your life, and how you turned around and created good for so many people. You helped thousands of people in your lifetime, even through your grief. I come from an incredibly strong line of badass women. And I'm sitting here losing sleep over a man I knew centuries ago in another lifetime? It's embarrassing, if I'm to be honest," Grace shrugged, getting to the root of the matter.

"Even strong women need support. A tree can't stand without its roots. Your roots are all of us, and you need to lean on us before you topple," Fiona said, her eyes full of love as she looked at Grace.

"I'm used to figuring things out on my own."

"I know you are, Gracie. Since the moment you were born, you've done things your way and your way only. You've gotten your way through charm, magick, arguing, and every other tactic in the book. You're headstrong, brilliant, and have a huge heart. It is no surprise to me that you once ruled the coasts with an iron fist as our famous pirate queen. But have you considered that perhaps you're being too hard on yourself?"

"I... I can't quite say." Grace shrugged once more.

"Maybe instead of trying to will the dreams away, you need to learn what the message is. For not everything can bend to your will – not even your own subconscious. I suggest you stop trying to force it and instead go within and ask what the message is."

"I suppose..." Grace said, grumpy from lack of sleep and from not having an easy solution to her problem. "Or I could just drink a bit too much of the Irish and sleep peacefully."

"That's an option, but I suspect not the solution to your problem," Fiona twinkled at her from across the table.

"Fine. But I'm still having a wee sip before bed because I like the taste and it's lovely to have by the fire at night," Grace grumbled.

Fiona held up her hands in agreement.

"You've no arguments from me on that front."

CHAPTER 3

The afternoon slipped by in a cozy blur of stories of the past, instructions from Fiona on tweaking a few of her magickal recipes for some of the elixirs Grace was working on, and the warm glow of spending time doing something she loved. She knew she was putting off going to sleep when Rosie nudged her head against Grace's leg once more.

The fire had drawn low, and aside from a few candles she had lit, Grace sat in darkness. The darkness never bothered her overmuch. It was hard to surprise her, let alone scare her. Her senses – both physical and psychic – were so heightened that anything that went bump in the night was quickly identifiable.

"I want the night. Before sleep, Rosie. I must have the night," Grace said, finishing her single pour of whiskey and standing from the chair to stretch and work the mild aches from her neck and back, the result of hunching over a table all day.

Stepping from the cottage, Grace inhaled the scents of

damp earth and salt carried to her on the breeze. It whipped along the ocean and danced over the cliffs, strong enough to fling her braid back over her shoulder, and causing her to wrap a scarf more firmly over her neck. The moon, a mere crescent of light in the sky, cast a dim pallor across the hills that rolled to the cliff's edge. Waves crashed far below, the sound of the ocean meeting the stark shoreline as soothing as a lullaby to Grace.

Oh, but she loved it here. Some would find the silence maddening, or be bored by the lack of things to do, but that wasn't the case for Grace. Cities could drive her to the brink of sensory overload with their hustle and bustle, their constant noises and annoyances. With her heightened psychic capabilities, car horns and the rush of people's thoughts and emotions were an attack on her senses that was almost too much to bear. She'd learned, over the years, how to shield herself from the onslaught of stimuli, but it always proved to be exhausting for her.

But not in this space. Letting her shields down, Grace danced her way across the dark field, allowing herself to feel the fabric of the universe around her. Even at night, the colors popped to her: The green of fresh spring grass, the budding of a bloom on a bush, the velvet blue of the night sky all created a lush painting worthy of the masters. Music –to her at least – came on the brush of the wind on her face, the singing of leaves fluttering in the breeze, the percussion of the waves crashing on the rocks, the humming of insects at night, all creating nature's most beautiful symphony. Grace loved the night, for she could see and feel what others could not – and it sang to her soul in ways that nothing else could.

Grace found herself standing on the edge of the cliffs that hugged the cove in an almost perfect half-circle, irresistibly drawn there as she had been so many centuries before. Though she lived in the now, her memory of a past time was stronger here, at the edge of the cove that she had made her own and had protected with her very own blood magick.

She could still feel that day – that moment – when she'd enchanted the cove. Using a strong ritual that required her to give up her life in exchange for the greater good, she'd blessed her bloodline with powerful magick and had protected her final resting place. At least, she'd thought it was final at the time.

Grace smiled down at the dark waters, the moonlight unable to reflect there, and shook her head at her silliness. Even as powerful as she was, Grace still had to admit that she didn't know – hadn't known – it all. It appeared that 'final' was never really final; Fiona's continued presence in Grace's life was a testament to that fact.

Closing her eyes, Grace let herself feel the hum of the universe. She allowed its energy to flow into her and took a deep breath.

"My angels, my Goddess, I ask you for your help in showing me the meaning of the dream I continue to have. I understand that I'm missing a message. Please guide me this night, as I walk through my dreams and visit lovers of centuries past."

That would have to do, Grace thought. Opening her eyes, she blew a kiss to the cove and sauntered back to where her cottage stood, the dim light from the candles still lit inside beckoning to her from across the hills. She whistled to Rosie – who loved to race across the grass, but loved bedtime even more – and laughed as the dog beat her to the door, tail wagging in delight.

"Yes, you've earned yourself a biscuit before bed," Grace said, going to the cheerful blue ceramic treat jar with dogs painted on it and pulling out a treat. Rosie's eyes never left the treat as Grace held it in front of her.

"Lock up," Grace ordered and Rosie raced to the door and pulled the rope Grace had attached to the latch so that the dog could lock the door each night. Once she'd pulled it closed, Rosie ran to each candle and carefully huffed out a breath which sounded almost like a sneeze to put the candles out. The dog stopped in front of the stove and cocked her head, her signal that she'd stay there until Grace came to inspect that the coals were down and there was no chance of fire.

"Good girl," Grace said, and gave an overjoyed Rosie the treat while she made sure the stove was secure. It was a silly little routine they had at bedtime, but when Grace had discovered just how smart Rosie was, she'd learned quickly that the dog liked having little tasks to accomplish through the day. She supposed she was a working dog, as Irish setters were known to be. Sometimes Grace sent her across the fields to Grace's childhood home, to go along with Flynn on a fishing outing or to visit the animals in the stables. It wasn't a bad life for a dog, Grace mused.

Nor for herself, either, she thought as she readied herself for bed. Her work fulfilled her, she had a lovely family, if she was bored she had but to nip into the village and have a pint at the pub with friends, and she always had books for company on stormy nights. Or Fiona would drop in to check on her.

So why was she feeling so lonely these days? Grace hugged her arms around herself after she climbed into bed, smiling as Rosie propped her paws at the end of the bed and looked at her.

"Go on then, you know you want to come up." Grace smiled and Rosie hopped up, circling three times before curling into a ball at the foot of the bed, always close by if needed.

Grace had taken the same room her mother, Keelin, had slept in when she'd first moved to Ireland from the States, before she'd met Grace's father. It just felt strange to sleep in Fiona's room, especially considering the old woman was still virtually living there, and Grace secretly loved the smaller guestroom – hers now – and the way the bed was tucked under the beams directly under the window. She had but to nudge the lace curtains aside in the morning and slide the window open to have what felt like the whole world at her feet. Some days she would kneel there, her body half hanging out the window as she watched the gulls dive far down the cliffs into the waves, or a fat bee buzz lazily by on the quest for its next flower. This room, sparse in decoration but huge in charm, was for dreamers – and above all else, Grace was a dreamer.

Now if only she could find the answer in one particular dream.

Sighing, she pulled the covers up and began the process of easing herself into sleep, slowly letting her thoughts go until she moved into the softness of her dreams. There, he waited, as she knew he would, once more laughing to her from the shoreline.

"Aye, there she is, my pretty Gráinne," Dillon said, his eyes alight with love and welcome.

The same feeling of insurmountable love washed over her, staggering her with its welcome, and she found herself once again smiling shyly at the man as he came forward to wrap his arms around her. Like a drug, she needed his kiss and leaned into it, feeling the same rush as she always did. Helpless to stop the dream – nor did she want to – Grace allowed herself to be carried inside, where the lovers redis-covered each other once again. After, instead of looking out to the horizon as she always did, Grace turned to Dillon, pressing her hand to his face.

"What worries you, my beauty?" Dillon asked, turning his mouth to kiss her palm.

"Why do I keep having this dream? What is your message for me? I worry for you," Grace said, changing the script a bit this time to see what he would say.

Dillon smiled, brushing his lips over hers in a kiss so tender that Grace's heart ached to hold him – just this once – in real life.

"You'll have this moment, forever, here in your heart. Once a love like ours is known, it can never be taken from us, and transcends all barriers – those of mortal law, those of time, and beyond what most can comprehend. It's an endless love, one that grows through the ages, and we'll meet, time and time again, our souls knowing each other, our love binding us for centuries. Be it but weeks of time in this lifetime, know that we're promised for more,

Gráinne O'Malley, for it is written in the tapestry of the universe."

"I know, Dillon. So you've said, many a time. I just… I wish you were near. That you could answer my questions," Grace said, pouting as the threads of the dream began to unravel and consciousness started to claim her.

"I'm here, my beautiful Gráinne. I'm here," Dillon said, his eyes laughing at her as she snapped awake. The dream splintered at her feet and she was left, once again, gasping for breath as sadness washed over her.

"If only that were true," Grace said, and wiped away the single tear she had allowed to spill from her cheek. "I so wish you were here."

CHAPTER 4

There was no way around it. Grace was in a mood and there wasn't anything to be done about it except try and avoid human interaction. She'd already responded harshly to an email from a blogger who wanted to interview her on the history of Grace's Cove and had asked if Grace would comment on the rumors of a curse that surrounded the sacred waters.

"The idiot doesn't know the first thing about magick. And she's going to try and write about it? That's how the wrong information gets spread," Grace grumbled, slamming her laptop closed and then immediately regretting it when Rosie whined gently at her feet.

"Sorry, baby," Grace said, reaching down to scratch Rosie's ears as she took a few deep breaths and tried to work her way through her funk. She'd been in a huff all morning – whether from the lack of answers or lack of sleep, she wasn't entirely sure. There was just something about this day that felt bad to her, and she really didn't want to deal with it. To amuse herself and Rosie, she focused on the dog's tennis ball, which sat in a basket across the room. With a quick mental shove, she sent the ball hovering into the air, much to the delight of Rosie who raced across the room and leapt to try and nip it from the air. This game never failed to cheer them both up, and it also served to keep Grace's telekinesis skills sharp.

Fiona had told her that the first time she'd used this particular skill of hers, she'd been only about six months old and had desperately wanted a stuffed lamb that had been sitting across the room from her crib. Apparently, her mother had been given quite the fright when the lamb had sailed through the air and hit Grace directly in the face. Grace chuckled at the image, glad she'd honed her skills through the years to exert a bit more control over her magick.

And, oh, what she'd learned through the years! With teachers like Fiona and Keelin to gently curb her enthusiasm, Grace had taken to all things magickal like a fish to water, and had soon eclipsed both her mother's and great-grandmother's abilities. Which made things a bit tricky during her rebellious teen years, when she was determined to do whatever she wanted, whenever she wanted. Not that much had changed since those rocky times, but at least she'd learned a touch more decorum in how to go about getting her own way.

Nonetheless, she still got what she wanted. Grace smiled and let the ball drop so that Rosie could finally reach it. She supposed it was probably her greatest flaw, but she liked to think of it as a strength. There was nothing wrong with being a strongminded woman who knew what she wanted. Assertive, Fiona had called her. Others had suggested she should be less combative, and for them she smiled sweetly and charmed them so completely they forgot they'd ever called her combative and barely noticed that she'd still managed to get her own way.

Not all charms had to be magickal.

Fiona had warned her that someday she'd run across someone or something she couldn't magick or charm her way out of, but she had yet to see it. Until then, she'd continue on her path, following in Fiona's and Keelin's footsteps of healing those in the village who needed it and working on an all-natural apothecary line that she'd signed a deal to distribute at a few exclusive natural-health stores in the States. She'd yet to tell anyone of the deal, wanting to get her brand and packaging down first before throwing a little launch party for it at Cait's pub. Just the thought of her new brand cheered her up and soon she was humming around the cottage as she dug out her folder of logo designs.

When the knock came at the door, Grace was so deep into her work that it took her a moment to realize that the knocking had persisted for quite a while and that Rosie was frantic with wanting to know who was on the other side of the door.

"Och, calm down, Rosie. We'll be seeing who's behind the door soon enough," Grace said, glancing down to make sure she was presentable. It wasn't uncommon for her to wander about the cottage in panties and a tank top, but today she'd pulled on loose jeans and an old jumper the color of moss.

Pulling the latch, she ordered Rosie to sit and opened the heavy wooden door – worn with age, but sturdy nonetheless – and blinked at the man standing outside with a folder in his hand.

"Good day, may I help you?" Grace said, and immediately felt the impending wave of doom she'd been fighting off all day slam into her. This man was here with anything but good news. Fighting to control her expression, Grace scanned the man – from his expensive loafers, which were entirely unsuitable for the countryside, all the way up his three-piece suit to his shrewd eyes tucked behind wire-framed glasses. His demeanor invited her to trust him. Grace trusted only her instincts.

"Ms. Grace O'Brien?" the man asked politely.

"Aye, 'tis myself. And you'd be?" Grace asked, crossing her arms and leaning casually against the door-frame, deliberately drawing out a thicker country accent for him. She wanted to see if he would treat her any differently.

"Ah, the name is Aiden Doherty. I've been employed by DK Sailing Enterprises," Mr. Doherty cleared his throat and gestured lightly with the papers in his hand.

"Sure and it's grand to be employed by a corporation and all, but could you be telling me what for?" Grace said, injecting some sass into her words. She saw the man flush before swallowing audibly once more and raising the papers in his hand. Whatever bad news he was about to drop on her, Grace wanted him to just say it.

"I'm their solicitor. They've requested that I come and serve you these papers formally announcing your eviction from this property, effective immediately. You've thirty days to vacate the premises along with all of your belongings."

For the first time in her life, Grace was at a complete loss for words. Not even when Fiona had died had Grace been as shocked as she was now, standing there while Mr. Doherty continued to fumble his way through an explanation. His words were lost to the wind that had kicked up in anger from the cove – or perhaps it was her own anger – and he clutched his coat together and bent forward into the wind, his grasp tightening on the folder of papers.

"If I could just pass this on to you…" Mr. Doherty gasped as a gust of wind ripped the hat from his head and sent it tumbling across the hills, a joyful Rosie racing after it. "All the information you need is here."

"I'm certain there's been some mistake," Grace said, her voice like sweet wine. She took the folder from Mr. Doherty but didn't open it. "This house and the land has been in my family for generations."

"Aye, I understand and I'll be issuing my apologies. It seems there was a lease that expired upon the death of…" Mr. Doherty paused as he searched for the name. "…Fiona O'Brien. The long-lease right of use ran out at her death. As nobody from the family filed to once more lease the land, technically it became open for public, um, consumption."

It would have been worse if he'd been mean about it. But Grace could tell that he felt slightly embarrassed at having to deliver such news. Reaching out with her mind, she scanned his brain and found a conflicting slew of emotions. He hadn't expected to find a woman alone here – much less one as pretty as she was – and now felt horrible for delivering such news. On top of it, he'd apparently heard the rumors of magick that filled the cove, and the increase of the wind had him speculating that she was a witch. More than anything he wanted to turn tail and run.

"I'm certain there's been a mistake. Thank you for delivering the papers to me. I'll have my own solicitor look these over this afternoon. Please tell DK Enterprises that they'll need to search for another, more suitable piece of property for whatever it is they plan to do here," Grace said and whistled sharply for Rosie. The dog raced across the land and dropped Mr. Doherty's hat, now mangled and slobbery, at his feet.

"Good luck to you, Miss O'Brien. You'll need it," Mr. Doherty said. Gingerly picking up his hat between two fingers, he all but ran back to his late-model sedan, the wind making him walk at an angle. Grace briefly considered giving him a flat tire on the way home, but realized there was no reason to hurt the messenger.

It was DK Enterprises she'd need to ruin.

CHAPTER 5

A world cruise, Grace fumed as she shot off a hysterical email to her mother. Of all the times... Her parents had decided to up and take a four-month world cruise and had left the stables, Flynn's restaurants, and his multitude of other businesses in the very capable hands of his manager. Which did little to help her now, Grace thought, as she stalked to her room to change clothes and try – though it wasn't likely to be successful – to calm herself down. Anger wasn't what was needed now, Grace reminded herself. Cool heads always prevailed and anger rarely won anything but enemies.

Grace desperately wished she could be one of those women who cruised through life with serenity and a smile, their boat never seeming to be overly rocked by much. Instead, Grace very much belied her name by having a tempestuous personality and moods that changed lightning-quick. She inhaled slowly and deeply as she pulled on snug black pants, along with a bright red jacket that always made her feel powerful. With a quick and somewhat unsteady hand she applied a touch of makeup, grabbed the folder from the table, and whistled for Rosie to come with her to her truck. The town had quickly grown used to Rosie accompanying Grace pretty much everywhere, and the cheerful dog was welcome at all businesses – including the one she now barreled her truck towards.

She took the winding curves of heart-stopping cliff road with a ruthless efficiency that came from years of practice. Storm clouds gathered on the horizon, an angry grey, most likely because Grace was having incredible difficulty reining her mood in. That meant her shields were down, and the storm clouds followed her into the small village of Grace's Cove, casting shadows and fat drops of rain on what had just been a singularly sunny day for the Irish village. Children raced inside as mothers banged windows shut against the sudden onslaught of the storm and Grace arrived at the doorstep of her solicitor in a huff, glaring at the rain that now pounded the windshield of her truck.

"I've brought this one on myself, haven't I then?" Grace said, letting out another beleaguered sigh before forcing herself to take deep breaths. As she calmed herself down, she brought an image into her mind of the clouds clearing, and worked on running a spell that would gently blow the storm on so she wouldn't have to arrive dripping wet in the waiting room of the very precise and somewhat pretentious Martin Wedgewick, Solicitor at Law. Grace didn't mind the pretention, as the man was fastidious with his work and had earned his reputation fairly. But she did mind his overly formal waiting room, which needed more charm and less of a 'don't muck up the furniture' attitude.

He had never outright forbade Rosie from visiting with Grace when they met to go over contracts for her apothecary line, but the little twitch over his eye when her happy-go-lucky dog barreled through the door was all she needed to know about how Martin Wedgewick, Solicitor at Law, felt about her dog in his office. However, it seemed the man had more restraint than Grace did when it came to speaking his mind, and he was wise enough to look the other way when a paying client, albeit a slightly odd and highly moody one, decided to drop in his office unannounced.

"Martin!" Grace said, having dashed inside with Rosie just as the rain cleared. His secretary, Anne, must have been out to lunch, and the man himself popped his head out of his office with a startled look on his face.

"Grace? Did we have an appointment?" Martin's glance slid over a wagging Rosie and confusion crossed his face as he looked over the shoulder of his neatly pressed herringbone jacket to his office.

"No, we didn't. But I simply must speak to you now. I have an extremely urgent problem. You see –" Grace slammed her mouth shut as her brain picked up on another mental signature in the office, and she realized that Martin wasn't alone. For once in her life, Grace kept her mouth shut as a slightly disheveled Anne came out of Martin's office.

"Filing's all done, Mr. Wedgewick. It looks like your appointment book is open until three o'clock today, so you'll have time to see Ms. O'Brien," Anne said, smoothly tucking a loose lock of warm brown hair into her low bun. She'd just gone from mousy secretary to interesting woman, in Grace's opinion, but there was no time to dwell on this delicious nugget of gossip.

"Thanks, Anne. You're a doll," Grace said, shooting her a beaming smile which caused Anne to smile back in return. Woman to woman they nodded at each other, nothing else needing to be said, and Grace continued into Martin's office.

The solicitor hastily tidied his desk. "Ah, Grace. You look a bit distraught. May I get you a cup of tea?" Martin asked, his gaze sliding toward the door once more.

"No, it's whiskey I'll be needing, but not yet. For now, I need a clear head," Grace said. She dropped the folder on his desk, turned to close the door behind them, and plopped herself into his visitor's chair.

"And what precisely would you need me to be looking at then?" Martin asked, crossing his fingers over the folder and pressing his lips tightly together. Grace did her best to keep her mental shields up as an image of her fussy solicitor and his timid secretary entangled in a kiss flashed through her head.

"I'm being evicted!" Thunder crashed outside once again, startling Martin. He glanced toward his window and Grace forced herself to tone it down before a hurricane swept up the coast because of her mood.

"I'm not sure I understand…" Martin said, refocusing on Grace and neatly sliding the papers from the envelope. "I was under the impression that your family owned the cottage you now live in."

"They do. My great-grandfather built that cottage for Fiona. The land has been in the O'Brien family for generations," Grace said, clasping her hands together in her lap and trying to calm herself as rain pelted the window. Fiona had tried for years to teach Grace to harness the effect her moods had on the outside world, and she'd thought she'd grown out of these types of responses. However, Grace felt dangerously close to losing control and it seemed all bets were off the table as thunder shook the building once more.

"DK Enterprises," Martin murmured, scanning the documents, pausing to look up into the air as though he was flipping through a file in his brain for more information. "I believe they own sailing charters. Or build boats. Something to do with sailing."

"Aye, his solicitor mentioned something of the sort. I don't care if this is the Pope. I'm not leaving my cottage. They'll need to bodily remove me," Grace threatened, then froze. "They can't be there right now, can they? Going through my stuff? Should I run home?" Stupid, stupid, stupid, Grace berated herself. She'd run out the door without leaving any level of magickal protection or even a stronger sturdy lock on her door.

"Ms. O'Brien," Martin said patiently, and then in a move unusual for him, he reached across the desk and squeezed her hand. Perhaps it was the uncharacteristic gesture or the sympathy on his face that broke Grace, but tears spiked her eyes as she waited to hear what she knew was coming. "Grace. I'm sorry, but these papers do seem to be in order. That doesn't mean that we can't fight them. The lease lapsed several years ago, but I believe we can make a case for your owner's rights – or even the fact that there doesn't seem to have been any sort of public notif-ication about the land being available. I will file a tempo-

rary injunction to stop this eviction – at the very least that
will grant us some time to determine the legalities of this
transaction. In the meantime, I suggest you do your best to
remain calm and we'll spend some time looking into this
DK Enterprises."

"I will ruin them," Grace declared, and a faint wisp of
a smile passed across Martin's face.

"That's not exactly what I had in mind when I
suggested you remain calm."

"Just work your magick and I'll work mine," Grace
said, standing. Then on impulse she bent and brushed a
kiss across Martin's cheek, causing the man to blush
faintly. "I like Anne; she's good for you. If I were you, I'd
take her out on a real date. Maybe buy her some flowers.
No woman likes to be kept behind closed doors."

With that she whistled for Rosie, leaving a startled
Martin behind her as she blew out the front door with a
quick wave for Anne. The last thing she heard as the door
closed behind her and she ducked into the pouring rain was
Martin stuttering through an invitation to dinner.

At least that was one good deed she'd done today.

CHAPTER 6

*G*race went where everyone in town went when they had a serious problem – the pub. Sure, it was a place for music and a pint with friends, but it was also the social center of the village and all gossip was meticulously dished out and dissected by the regulars who graced the stools there. Despite herself, Grace wished Cait's daughter, Fi, hadn't taken off on a year abroad to find herself or whatever she was doing in this moment. She was the closest thing Grace had to a sister in this town, and she could have dearly used her guidance.

But the mother would do.

Cait's pint-sized frame manned the taps behind the long length of bar that dominated one end of Gallagher's Pub. Though there were other pubs sprinkled throughout Grace's Cove, this pub was truly the hub and the heart of the village. From births to deaths to weddings to graduations – a pint was raised by all, along with a session of music, to celebrate. And for the last thirty years, scrappy

Cait McAuliffe had run the pub with a cheerful efficiency that let everyone know she was boss.

Cait was like a second mum to Grace and spotted her distress from the moment Grace stepped through the door. By the time Grace had taken two steps, Cait had already ducked under the pass-through and was crossing the room to meet her with a hug. For a moment, Grace let herself be held and Cait rocked her gently, even though Grace towered over the diminutive woman.

"Do you want me to read you? Is it too hard to say?" Cait, ever respectful, usually did her best to shield her gift and stay out of reading people's minds. In her line of work, it'd be virtually impossible to get through a night behind the bar if she was constantly barraged with people's thoughts. With those close to her, Cait had made a promise to stay out of their heads unless asked. As far as Grace could tell, Cait stuck by that rule as a matter of honor. She was sure there were probably a few slip-ups here and there, as Grace struggled with the same issue with her magick.

"I'll be telling you, but I need a whiskey first," Grace said and crossed the room with Cait to settle on an empty stool. The storm had begun to drive locals in, for where else to go on a rainy afternoon but to the cozy pub to chat with friends over a wee pint and the cheerful flames from the fire in the corner? Even as Grace thought it, a man was stooping before the grate and lighting the peat that was always to be found there – as at home in the pub as if he owned it himself.

This was family, Grace thought, knowing all the faces in the bar and nodding to people from across the room. It was impossible to live her whole life in a town like this and not feel interwoven with all the people in the community.

"That's a pretty jacket, my Gracie girl," Mr. Murphy, ninety if he was a day, flirted with her from his stool at the end of the bar. "Someday you'll run away with me."

"Only if you'll be taking me to Jamaica and out of this rain, Mr. Murphy," Grace said.

Mr. Murphy threw his head back and laughed, slapping his hand on the bar top. "Too much sun for this fair skin, my dear heart. I wouldn't be wanting to get any more wrinkles."

Despite her mood, Grace laughed with him.

"Drink," Cait ordered, sliding a small glass of whiskey across the bar to Grace. She only raised an eyebrow when Grace downed it in one gulp, and continued to build the pints of Guinness she'd started. The whiskey burned straight to Grace's gut – as she'd wanted it to – and matched the flames of her mood.

"Have you heard of DK Enterprises? A sailing company?" Grace asked, pitching her voice just slightly over the din of chatter so anyone in the room could chime in if they wanted. It was an accepted way of inviting people with information or gossip to jump into the conversation; if she didn't want anyone involved, Grace would simply have turned away and spoken softly to Cait. For such a gossipy small town, the hushed voice and turned back was typically respected. For the most part, everyone knew they'd find out the gossip one way or another.

"Aye, the lad was just in the other day, wasn't he then, Cait?" Mr. Murphy asked, tugging on the newsboy cap that was perpetually tucked over the few strands of shock-white hair he still had. His eyes crinkled as he smiled at Grace. "Handsome lad at that, Gracie. You've got your eye on him then?"

"I've eyes only for you, Mr. Murphy, as you well know. No, I've never met the man nor know anything about this company of his," Grace said, taking a sip of the water Cait had put in front of her and drumming her fingers on the bar.

"I've heard he's building here. A new development." This from a younger lad across the bar. "He's offered several job postings at a fair wage. Several of my mates have already applied."

"It was condominiums, I heard," another voice chimed in, and then the whole room started talking at once. The idea of a sleek unit of condos in their charming little village struck them all as wrong.

"Condos," Grace hissed, her shoulders slumping as she considered this new development. "Why would a sailing man build condos?" The thought of her beautiful cottage and the lovely emptiness of the green hills surrounding it being bulldozed to build condo units made fury churn low in her belly.

"It's always smart to diversify your income. I presume the lad saw a need. He seemed nice enough," Mr. Murphy said, seeming unperturbed at the news. He'd been around long enough to know that these things took time and often sorted themselves out. If the people of Grace's Cove decided they didn't want condos, they'd find a way to keep them out.

"What's this about, Grace?" Cait asked, her voice soft

as she topped off her pints of Guinness and left them to settle before starting the process of the next ones.

"It seems I'm being evicted," Grace said, careful to try and keep her emotions in check lest she bring a monsoon down upon poor Gallagher's Pub.

There had been very few moments like this one in the pub, when nothing could be heard but glasses slamming onto tables in surprise and the howling of the wind outside. The Irish were known for their words, and it wasn't often that an entire group was at loss for any.

"You're what?" Cait exclaimed, her face passing through six different emotions so rapidly that Grace could barely keep up with them. "I'll kill them. Who's done this to you?"

Grace gestured with her hand and said nothing, letting Cait reach her own conclusion.

"DK Enterprises? They want to build the condos there? On..." Cait gasped as it really hit home, and slapped her hand to her heart. "Over Fiona's cottage?"

Grace nodded sullenly, continuing to do her best to keep control over the rage that threatened to bubble over.

"No. This can't happen. We'll stop this from happening. There must be some mistake. You own that land," Cait said, nodding smartly as the chatter resumed in the pub, everyone drawing their own conclusions about what was happening.

"It seems the long-lease use of land expired when Fiona passed." Grace didn't like to say that Fiona had died, as the old woman still was very much present in their lives. She knew for a fact that Fiona popped into Cait's thoughts for a chat more often than the pub owner cared for.

"That can't be right. And this DK Enterprises just bought it and evicted you?" Cait clarified.

"Yes. The solicitor showed up at my doorstep this very morning, and politely requested that I move out."

"I hope you sent the bum running!" another villager cried out from across the room. Grace's temper was well known in the village and the majority had decided it was far more enjoyable to stay on her good side. Being on Grace's good side felt like turning your face to the sun. It was best not to speak of her bad side.

"That I did," Grace said, and nodded down to Rosie. "And Miss Rosie made sure his hat was hardly wearable."

"That's a good pup," Cait said, tossing a treat over the bar. Rosie caught it in mid-air and then circled the room as the people whistled for her, to be petted and congratulated on her fine job of protecting her mum.

"We'll stop him," Cait said, meeting Grace's eyes dead on.

"Aye, that we will. DK Enterprises has no idea who they are messing with."

CHAPTER 7

*D*ylan Kelly surveyed the storm ravaging the wide harbor at the base of Grace's Cove. He'd spent much of his life on the water, and a bit of weather never fussed him much. The suddenness of this storm surprised him, though; it was as if it had appeared from thin air. He made a note to look at the weather patterns for Grace's Cove and see if this was a usual occurrence, as it could affect his future plans here.

Grace's Cove, Dylan thought, as he pressed his palms to the window and let his gaze sweep over the little village nestled in the hills on the water. If he were a fanciful man, he'd have said this place had called to him his whole life. While the sailor side of him appreciated whimsy and lore, for the most part Dylan remained a pragmatic and driven businessman. It suited him to do what he loved for a living – being on the water – but having decided to forego the struggles of a fisherman's life, Dylan had also followed his other love.

Making money.

He had married his two loves into a successful sailing enterprise – which ran everything from cargo vessels that shipped all over the world to luxury charters that cruised through the Mediterranean – and Dylan was a man who was content with his life.

Content, Dylan thought as he pursed his lips, until he hadn't been. His mother had repeatedly reminded him that a successful life was nothing without love. Typically, Dylan would distract her with stories from his latest travels before she moved on to pointing out her lack of grandchildren. Though he loved his mother dearly, he knew that she wasn't entirely fond of his admittedly playboy ways. She'd tolerated it in his twenties, but now that he was well into his thirties, she'd decided enough was enough.

In his own way, so had Dylan. The excitement of a new woman each month or in different countries had quickly worn off and now he yearned for something else – a deeper commitment, he supposed. Or at the very least, being able to trust the woman he chose to bed.

Dylan raked his hand through his tawny blond hair, left to grow too long once again, and moved away from the window of the house he'd rented in the hills overlooking the village. The last woman he'd dated longer than a few months had turned out to be much like the rest, interested in what his money could buy her and nothing more than that. Sure and he was a generous sort – having a great love of women and believing they deserved frivolous gifts – but after a time he'd begun to wonder if anyone enjoyed his company simply for who he was as a person. It had been ages since he'd brought anyone new into his confidence, and even longer since he'd properly dated.

Though his mother had been delighted to see him giving up his dalliances with the model of the month, she'd grown more concerned over the past eighteen months as he had ceased dating altogether.

"Not dating at all certainly isn't the way to find love," Catherine Kelly's words echoed in his mind.

"Dating hasn't found me love either," Dylan had parried, kissing her cheeks to soften his words.

"I worry for you," Catherine had said, allowing her son to embrace her.

"Don't worry. I'm just spending time focusing on my business." Dylan had kissed her once more on his way out.

Her words had followed him. "A lonely pursuit!"

Perhaps he was lonely, Dylan mused as he crossed to the bar tucked in the corner of the living room. In lieu of staying at a hotel, he'd rented an entire house, and was utterly charmed with his choice. Wood beams crisscrossed the ceiling, a beautiful stone fireplace hugged one wall, bookshelves lined another, and a beautifully woven rug in a brilliant shade of red was tossed across the wide planked floors. Deep leather couches and a state-of-the-art sound system completed the room and Dylan allowed himself to relax as he switched some music on and poured himself a whiskey, neat.

His eyes landed on the fireplace and then tracked back to where the storm continued its assault outside. If ever a day called for a whiskey, a fire, and a good book, it was this one. Crossing the room, he bent his tall frame before the fireplace, and in moments the first cheerful spurt of flame signaled he was well on his way to a delightfully comfortable lazy afternoon.

Pleased with himself and his decision to come here, Dylan bypassed the folder of papers for work – he'd deal with those in the morning. Instead, he pulled a Steinbeck novel off the bookshelf at random and soon lost himself in the words, allowing the restlessness that had been his companion of late to ease from his body.

It was that same restlessness that had led Dylan to Grace's Cove and to his latest venture. For the first time in ages he was truly excited about a new business project. If all went well, he'd be knee-deep in mud and building in a matter of weeks.

With any luck, this project should at least keep him too busy to think about his lack of a dating life, let alone about the strange pull he had to this town. The sailor in him would call Grace's Cove his destiny. The businessman in him would call it a smart decision.

Either way, Dylan hoped he was in for a fun ride.

CHAPTER 8

*S*till worked up after her time at the pub, Grace pulled in front of her Aunt Aislinn's gallery to see if she was still in the shop. Word had traveled quickly after Grace's bombshell, and the pub had filled as the story was repeated and more information on DK Enterprises was brought to light.

Which turned out to not be all that much, Grace thought with disgust as she turned off her motor and peeked through the wall of rain to see if any light shone from the wide front window of the gallery. The most the villagers had been able to agree upon was that the company ran sailing charters, was building something here – likely condos – and that none of the villagers would work for the man if he was truly tearing down Fiona O'Brien's cottage. Grace wondered if that last part was true, for a decent living wage was something that came dear to many of the people of the village. While Grace's Cove was relatively well-functioning, it relied largely on tourism and the fishing industry. Grace knew that many of the families struggled over the long cold winter months, when tourists rarely ventured this far west and fishermen struggled with near impossible conditions. It was one thing to make a promise of turning away work after downing a pint in the pub, and another to turn away work when there were mouths to feed at home.

Still, just the thought of any of the villagers knowingly trying to bulldoze her cottage had lightning shocking across the sky and thunder rattling the gallery. When the door swung open and an angry Aislinn glared at her through the curtain of rain, Grace hunched her shoulders and mouthed "Sorry" through the glass. Calming herself, she waited for the rain to dissipate slightly before whistling to Rosie and making a dash from her truck to the front door.

"I don't think so with that wet mutt. Around back," Aislinn ordered, slamming the door in Grace's gaping face.

"Shite, I had to make it storm," Grace swore, and splashed through puddles until she reached the back gate that surrounded a little courtyard. She pushed herself inside and raced through the back door until she stood, rain streaming from her hair, in the back room of Aislinn's gallery.

Aislinn eyed Grace critically before handing her a towel and motioning for her to join her in her office. An acclaimed artist, Aislinn's office was anything but conventional; her flowing dress, tumbling hair, and the riot of necklaces and bracelets that jingled as she walked echoed that. Grace followed her, being careful to dab away the wet, and ran the towel over Rosie for good measure. The last thing she needed was Aislinn squealing at her if Rosie shook water on some precious artwork or relic that she had tucked away in her office.

"Hi, Gracie." Morgan, who had been a team with Aislinn for as long as Grace could remember, called to her from where she worked behind a laptop at the wide dining table that was being used as a desk. Aislinn and Morgan shared a special bond – as much best friends as they were family. Taking Morgan under her wing years ago as a shop girl had been one of the best decisions Aislinn had ever made. Together, they'd made their business blossom and now ran one of the most acclaimed galleries in all of Ireland.

And both were magick.

At home here, Grace plopped into a wide leather chair with worn cushions and pretty paisley pillows. Crossing her legs, she let out a long beleaguered sigh.

"Hiya, Morgan and Aislinn. I've had a hell of a day," Grace said.

Morgan nodded toward the little iPhone sitting by her computer. "We've just heard. Cait rang us from the pub. We were going to come out to the cottage after the storm, but got the message you were on your way."

It wasn't Cait who had given them the message, Grace mused, as she'd told no one where she was going. But living with magick and the flow of the natural rhythms of the universe with her friends and family made it easy to communicate in other ways than via telephone.

"I should probably get back there before the bulldozers roll up," Grace grumbled, though she knew it would be some time before a digger showed up. If only she could wrap her mind around just how she would handle this situation.

"You don't really think they'll level the cottage, do you? There has to be a way to stop this," Morgan protested, her gorgeous face creased with concern.

"I have Martin Sedgewick working on it. He said he'll try and file an injunction to stop any of this nonsense, at least until we can get it sorted out," Grace said.

"I like him," Aislinn noted as she poured tea at the sideboard. "He's fussy, but diligent. I suspect he'll handle things well."

"I caught him kissing Anne," Grace said, delighted to have a reason to gossip now. She was safe here – she'd never spread that type of gossip in the pub. But with family, they could have a good chat and keep her mind off of her troubles.

"No!" Morgan's eyes lit up with excitement. "I never would have guessed."

"That's… Why, actually, I think they'd be perfect for each other," Aislinn mused as she delivered tea in chunky mugs, glazed in a misty blue color, which Grace knew she'd made herself.

"I thought the same. I gave him a little nudge to take her out to a real dinner instead of hiding behind doors. I heard him asking her on my way out," Grace said, feeling slightly cheered at the thought of two people on the brink of finding love.

"You look tired," Morgan said, her beautiful eyes searching Grace's face. "When did you find out about this? Has it been keeping you up at night?"

"I found out just today, so no, it hasn't been keeping

me up. I... I don't know. I keep having those dreams again. They seem to be intensifying. I wish there was a way to magick my brain to forget them – to forget him. Despite my best efforts, I've come up with nothing. Fiona's only given me the advice on asking what I'm supposed to learn in the dream. So far she refuses to give me a way to actually get rid of the dreams. I swear the old woman takes joy in watching me suffer," Grace said, rolling her eyes at the women though they knew she was just joking. They all knew that Fiona had never liked to watch her chicks suffer, but if there were lessons to be learned – well, they had to learn them.

"You haven't found the answer, then," Aislinn said, her hand toying with an amethyst amulet that hung low at her waist. "What are you ignoring?"

Grace shrugged a shoulder and sipped her tea as she considered the question. The storm continued to blow outside, but she was cozy and comfortable here, so she settled into silence for a moment and let her mind wander.

"My guess is that I'm supposed to believe in love, since the dreams all focus on me reliving love and then losing it."

"Or maybe it's about the fact that you can't always get exactly what you want?" Morgan piped up, then flushed when they turned to look at her. Even after all these years and all the confidence Morgan had developed, she still had moments of insecurity when all the attention turned to her.

"How so?" Aislinn demanded.

"It just seems like this constant cycle of Grace reliving this beautiful time in a past life and then having it torn from her. She's repeatedly stated that she wants that love or wants this man in her life… one way or the other. And nothing changes. But she hasn't changed her approach and her dreams haven't changed. So I'd say, from a bird's-eye view, it comes across to me as Grace wanting things done her way and she's on this hamster wheel of dreams until she relinquishes… something. Perhaps her demands that the dream be over? Or that she have this love? I'm not completely sure and that's the truth of it," Morgan said and then took a slug of tea to shut herself up.

"I… Well, hmmm. That could be true. I suppose. Fiona does like to say I've always gotten whatever I've wanted in life and someday I'll run up against something I can't have," Grace said, dropping her hand down to scratch Rosie's ears. "But that still doesn't make sense because it's just a dream about a past life. I can't go back and change that life; I can only fix this one. Anyway, to be totally honest, the dream doesn't even matter right now. The only thing that matters is what's about to happen with this DK Enterprises."

"Why does this worry me?" Aislinn asked, sliding a glance to Morgan as Grace got up, her face set in mutinous lines.

"Because I think our great pirate queen is about to go into battle," Morgan murmured as Grace disappeared into the storm.

CHAPTER 9

*F*or the first time in ages, Grace didn't dream of Dillon. Either it was the sheer rage that kept her tossing and turning and never falling fully into a deep sleep, or it was the storm that thundered through the night keeping her up – either way, Grace rose the next morning with the blood of battle in her eye.

Fiona had been surprisingly absent when Grace had returned home the night before, which had only served to annoy Grace even further. Sure, the old woman liked to pop in whenever she felt like – but when Grace needed her most? Not a peep. That just figured. Ghosts – finicky beings, they were.

She glanced out the window and was surprised to find that the weather had actually calmed down – not following her mood for once. A light breeze kissed the soggy grass and a few cotton-puff clouds graced the horizon. All in all, it should have been a lovely morning for Grace to make a cup of tea and get on with her work. Instead, she stood list-lessly in front of the sink, idly pushing the window open to catch the breeze, her face creased in a frown as her mind refused to quiet. At the moment, she saw no way out of the problem that currently presented itself to her.

Grace hated not having a way out.

In a concession to the chill in the air, Grace tugged a loose grey sweater over her tank and filmy sleep shorts, letting her hair tumble loose over her shoulders almost to her waist. It wasn't like she always had to have her way, Grace mused, as she put the kettle on to boil. She was more than capable of working with a team, and she'd had her share of boyfriends who would willingly have stayed with her if she hadn't danced lightly away from their offers of commitment. It was more about freedom – freedom of choice and freedom of movement. The fear – of not having a voice in her life or her choices – might have her labeled as a difficult woman.

It wasn't a label Grace minded.

The slamming of car doors and the sound of voices carried to her through the open window and had Grace's head going up as if she scented prey. Eyes narrowed, she edged to the window to find a trio of trucks, one towing some sort of construction machinery behind it, along the cliff road that led to the cove. Without a second thought, Grace bolted from the house, recognizing the outlet for her rage.

The group of men turned at Rosie's bark, signaling the arrival of an infuriated, barefoot, and half-dressed woman, her hair streaming behind her in the wind as she skidded to a stop in front of them. Assessing the look on her face, as one, the men turned to their leader.

Cowards, Grace thought, seeing the silent agreement

pass between the men as they decided to hand her off to the man who stood a bit apart from them, his back to her as he studied the waves that crashed far below where they stood. Broad shoulders covered by a worn leather jacket, ragged denim that hugged long legs, and blond hair – just beginning to curl – dancing in the wind. Grace could appreciate the build of the man while simultaneously wanting to throw him off the cliff.

"We'll start here then..." The man turned when his men remained silent and the shock of him caused Grace to lift a hand to her heart.

She couldn't see him. Not at first. The sun had risen far enough in the sky that it silhouetted his form, seeming to light his blond hair as it haloed around his head, his face momentarily lost in shadow. She caught it, just for a moment: the searing blue of his eyes – the ocean at dawn – before his face dropped back into shadow. The punch of him, of who he was, made her want to drop to her knees.

Instead, she straightened her shoulders and lifted her chin, leveling her gaze at him and swallowing past a throat that had gone achingly dry.

"Miss O'Brien, I presume?" The man stepped forward until he stood close to her, forcing her gaze to trail up a loosely-buttoned plaid to examine the face that she unequivocally wanted to kiss.

"Aye, 'tis me." Grace was distraught to hear her voice come out but a whisper on the wind. She wanted to scream the words. *'Tis me.* Couldn't he see?

His eyes narrowed as he studied her, and Grace frowned when annoyance flashed across his handsome features. With a jaw made for breaking a man's hand and soulful eyes that could make a weaker woman than Grace swoon, the man had the look of a fallen angel. A highly annoyed fallen angel, who glanced quickly at the neat wristwatch he wore and then back to where she stood, gaping like a lunatic, in her pajamas.

"It seems we've pulled you out of bed. I suppose it's best you get used to the construction as it will be only getting louder around here for a while yet."

"And with whom do I have the distinct displeasure of speaking?" Grace tilted her head, acid dripping from her tongue.

"My apologies. Dylan Kelly," he said, holding out a hand to shake and then dropping it when Grace looked at it like it was a snake poised to bite. "I understand you're unhappy with this situation. I promise we'll do our best to get you moved out with as little fuss as possible. DK Enterprises will be more than happy to pay for a moving van and help for you during your time of transition as well." Dylan rocked back on his heels, a placating smile hovering on his lips, dismissing her as a minor problem to be handled.

The man had no idea what he was in store for, Grace thought, drawing in one long shuddering breath. For once in her life, she needed to think with her mind and not her heart, as it seemed her heart currently couldn't be trusted to make wise decisions. If she followed the wave of emotions that swept through her right now, she'd have leapt into Dylan's arms and planted kisses across every inch of that stubborn jaw of his. And perhaps she still should, Grace thought, briefly entertaining the possibility of ruffling this man's feathers in a very unexpected way.

The problem was that he looked like the type who was used to women throwing themselves at him. It might unnerve or embarrass him, but Grace suspected it wouldn't throw him off his stride much. Instead, she sent his men a saucy smile that got her several answering smiles in return.

"Sure and that's right kind of you, Mr. Kelly, but I won't be needing your assistance as I'm not moving," Grace said, smiling sweetly as he arched a brow at her words.

"Is that so? Perhaps I've been misinformed. I was led to believe that you were notified of the eviction as well as the change of ownership of this land. I do apologize if this comes as a shock, I was certain that you'd been contacted," Dylan said, turning to look over his shoulder at one of the men who nodded at him in confirmation.

"Aye, I've been notified," Grace said, idly twisting a lock of hair around her finger, playing up the picture she was sure she currently presented – silly little dimwitted woman. Grace rarely used her looks for her own benefit, but she wasn't against playing into the assumptions men made about her if it got her what she wanted. Which, at the moment, was for them to get off her land.

"Ah, so, then... my offer stands," Dylan said, a lazy smile on his lips, his eyes sharp as he watched her.

"Sure and that's kind of you," Grace repeated. "But I'll not be moving. You will be."

Dylan shoved his hands into his pockets, a look of mild frustration fluttering across his face, and glanced back at his men, who collectively shrugged their shoulders as if to say she was his problem. Grace couldn't say why that annoyed her even more, but she decided then and there she'd teach them a little lesson. For if they wouldn't take no for an answer, she had other ways to change their minds.

"Miss O'Brien, I can understand that this is a bit distressing for you, but as your new landlord, I'm within my rights to evict you from the land," Dylan said, his voice dead calm, a man used to people obeying his orders.

"Mr. Kelly, as the current resident of this land, I'm telling you that you are wrong. This simply won't be the case," Grace said, her eyes boring into his, willing him to recognize her on any level. Something flashed in the depths of blue, but no recognition came to light. Instead, he pinched his nose and sighed.

"I don't have all day to stand here and argue with you. Here's my card. Call me to let me know when the moving van can come assist you," Dylan said, handing her a card. Grace readily took it, just to have something with his energy on it. She'd study it later, but for now she noted the jump in her pulse when his hand lightly brushed over her palm.

"You won't be receiving that call from me. My solicitor is filing an injunction against you, so for now, you're shut down. In the meantime, you'll want to be moving your equipment off of my land," Grace said, her chin up and fire in her eyes.

"Is that so? Interesting," Dylan murmured, pulling an iPhone out of his pocket and typing in a message. Grace briefly wondered how he got signal out here by the cliffs, and then shook her head to keep herself focused.

"Interesting, the man says. I see you're accustomed to getting your way. I'm sorry that your way won't work in this particular instance. But I'm certain there's loads of other coastline available in Ireland just begging for you to destroy it. Sadly – for you, certainly not for me – it won't be this cove. I'll have to be asking you once more to leave. I'd hate to bring the Garda out to assist you in your departure – Sheriff Maury with his new babe at home and all. I'm certain he'd be highly annoyed to be torn away from that to attend to a trespassing complaint." Grace smiled, widening her eyes and hoping she was pulling off the guileless look. "But I suppose that, since I did help his darling wife Deborah deliver their new babe, he'd be feeling obliged to protect me from any... threats to my property." Grace blinked up at Dylan, delighted to see that she'd finally worked her way under his cool exterior when anger flashed across his face.

Then he smoothed his expression out once more. "I'm certain there's no need for the authorities to come work out a simple misunderstanding," Dylan said, his tone pitched to match hers in sweetness. "But I promise you now – for every day you cost me in building, that's one less day you'll have to pack up your pretty little cottage over there."

"Is that a threat, Mr. Kelly?" Grace narrowed her eyes at him as she put her hands on her hips, refusing to budge from her position.

"I never threaten women, especially beautiful ones," Dylan said, a wide grin flashing across his face, surprising Grace into wanting to respond in kind. "I only make promises."

"You strike me as a man who is comfortable with

breaking his promises," Grace said, perhaps more sharply than intended.

Dylan's face went to stone. "I live by my word, Miss O'Brien. You'd do well to remember that," he said, his voice dangerously soft, forcing Grace to lean forward slightly to catch the words the rising wind threatened to carry away.

"As do I, Mr. Kelly. And I won't be bullied. Off with you now, off my land." Grace turned and made a shooing motion to the group of men, as if they were little more than pests to be done away with.

The group of men shuffled their feet, uncertain of what to do, all of them reluctant to lose face in front of their boss. Dylan only quirked a small smile at her, seemingly delighted with her motions. It was as though he was appeasing a country bumpkin or some batty old woman, and Grace felt rage flash through her when she realized he had no intention of taking her seriously.

The group of men started when, all at once, their car horns began honking on their own. Confused, they raced to their vehicles, only to jump back in shock when the doors flew open, beckoning them to jump inside. Grace swallowed a laugh while the men huddled together, the whites of their eyes showing in fear as the doors continued to open and close, the repetitive honking of the horns making it all but impossible to hear.

Only Dylan held his ground, his eyes narrowed and hands on his lean hips as he first watched the trucks and then slid a lazy glance back to her.

"That your work?" Dylan asked.

Grace was even more annoyed that he wasn't the least

bit concerned by the tiny display of magick she'd been unable to resist. "No sir," she said, lying as prettily as she could. "The land here's enchanted. You might want to do your research a bit more thoroughly before you pick your next spot to build. The spirits are obviously unhappy with you." With that, she turned and whistled for Rosie, who raced ahead of her across the grass toward the cottage – toward home. Grace refused to look behind her, knowing that if she did she'd find Dylan staring after her. She wouldn't give him the satisfaction.

She was delighted to hear the engines of the trucks roar to life as the men scurried from the cliffs. For this day, she'd won the battle.

But she knew there was still a war to fight.

CHAPTER 10

*D*ylan kept quiet as he tapped out a text message to his solicitor, demanding a call within the hour and an explanation for the current legal state of affairs on what he'd thought was now his land. Liam, his foreman and one of his closest friends, chattered incessantly at the wheel as he took the hairpin turns of the road that hugged the cliff on the way back into the village.

"What just happened? I've never seen anything like that. I'd heard, that I had – I was warned…" Liam shook his dark head of shaggy hair. "Down at the pub. They said the land was cursed or enchanted or whatever. But you know, Ireland, it's all magick, no? I figured it was just one of those things." Liam waved a hand in the air to illustrate his point.

"It's not magick," Dylan grumbled.

"Listen to himself, then. Telling me that's not magick. I know magick when I'm seeing magick, don't I? Car doors don't just open and close of their own accord," Liam said, tugging on a beard that had grown longer than he usually let it.

"Gust of wind," Dylan grumbled, propping one boot on his knee as he continued to work the computer in his hands.

"Hell of a gust of wind if you ask me. I'd say more like a gust of woman, no? One hell of a woman there, too." Liam whistled long and low, making Dylan get his back up. Which didn't even make sense – why should he care what Liam thought of Miss O'Brien?

"I'd say more like a hell of a problem. One that I don't have the time or the inclination for," Dylan said.

"It's a sad day when a man doesn't have the time or inclination for the likes of a woman like that. I think every man there fell more than halfway in love with her – either because of the way she stood up to you or the way she looked, or both. It's all of it. Some package," Liam said, a faint smile hovering on his lips as he replayed the scene in his head.

For the first time in their friendship, Dylan wanted to punch the man. Since the feeling shocked him, and he didn't deal well with being out of control of his emotions, Dylan forced himself to think back to the picture Grace O'Brien had made as she'd squared off to him on the cliffs.

Her face, flushed pink from the wind and her run across the grass, with her sunset hair tossing everywhere in the wind, had instantly made him think of a rumpled lover fresh from a tumble in bed. Her flimsy excuse for sleep shorts had barely covered her generous bum and curvy thighs. Dylan could only be grateful she'd had the forethought to pull a lumpy sweater over whatever else she was wearing – or perhaps not wearing – or she'd have had his entire crew kneeling at her feet. Her eyes, though – the deep blue ocean shade he'd only seen hours from land – had riveted him. If he was right, they changed color when she was angry, deepening to a midnight blue. Dylan wondered what they'd do when she was aroused.

He'd wanted to hug her. The thought alone had surprised him into acting even more cantankerous than he usually did. But there was something about Grace – almost a familiarity – that made him want to pull her into his arms and protect her from everything and anything that threatened to hurt her. Granted, she'd probably cosh him on the head if he tried to fix any problems for her, but the instinct was there nonetheless. Dylan decided it must be because he had a natural inclination toward being a problem solver, and he certainly didn't mind rescuing a damsel in distress when the occasion arose. Too bad that this time the person causing the damsel's distress was none other than himself.

Shaking his head away from such thoughts, he looked down at the phone that vibrated in his hand.

"She may be some package," Dylan agreed, knowing his friend would see through him if he tried to deny it, "but she's also some problem. One that I'm on the way to fixing."

"I look forward to watching that," Liam murmured, but Dylan had already tuned him out, the phone pressed to his ear as he began to discuss strategy.

CHAPTER 11

*I*t was him.

Grace curled into the rocking chair. It had been hand-carved with love, the edges worn smooth by the years of comfort taken by those who sat in it, whiling away the hours before the fire. Usually, the rocking soothed her, but today it only served to agitate her further.

Thump. Grace's foot hit the floor each time she rocked forward, her mind racing. How could Dillon be here – be this man – and not recognize her? It was impossible not to feel the connection between them. Wasn't it? He'd promised her that their love would transcend the bounds of time. And yet he'd stood there with barely a ripple of recognition on his too-handsome face and regarded her as nothing more than an annoying fly buzzing about his head.

That had stung, more than she'd wanted it to. Grace had been so caught up in the wave of emotions that plummeted through her when she'd first seen Dillon that she could only commend herself for sticking strong, staying in the moment, and kicking the man's decidedly delectable arse off her property. *Her* property. The man would learn soon enough that he was about to enter a battle of wills for which he had no training.

Pulling his card out, Grace studied the words.

Dylan Kelly, President. Ah, so that was what the DK stood for in DK Enterprises, Grace mused, noting that Dylan spelled his name differently in this life, though his initials remained the same. She would have to spend a little time researching his family line to see if she could find out anything more about what had happened to him through the years. Grace approved of the card; it was elegant, yet the pop of orange in the logo highlighted the neat navy-blue lettering. It was a smart choice, not just another boring business card. Unsure why that annoyed her even more, Grace closed her eyes and let the card sit in her palm as she went deep within.

A man used to getting his way, he had a soft spot for his mother. Grace smiled a bit as she read the energy from his card. It was clear that he had his walls up – though she couldn't tell if it was because he'd been hurt or if he had grown cautious through the years. His friends he kept near, his enemies closer, and a watchful eye on all his business enterprises. The man was strong, with a lightning-quick mind, a taste for good whiskey, and a heart that hadn't been fully touched yet. Grace wondered if he knew that he'd been waiting for her.

Which presented quite a problem, Grace thought as Rosie's wet nose nudged her knee and she popped her eyes open. Her enemy was the love she'd been waiting for, and now Grace had two battles to fight – one for her land and the other for her heart.

"He's quite the package," Fiona commented, making Grace thump both feet to the floor in surprise as Rosie raced across the room to circle the bench where the ghost sat.

"Damn you, old woman, haven't I told you to warn a body?" Grace complained, her heart thundering in her chest.

"No need for cursing," Fiona said primly, her eyes steely as she leveled a look at Grace. Grace knew that look, as did every one of her cousins and aunts and uncles.

"Sorry, ma'am," Grace said, hunching her shoulders in her seat.

"That's quite all right. It's been an understandably distressing day. I've been known to say some unsavory words meself." Fiona's eyes twinkled at Grace.

"That does not surprise me in the slightest," Grace murmured, bending down to give Rosie a proper pat. The dog wiggled in delight at her feet, always happy for a cuddle.

"You aren't the only firecracker around here, I'll have you know," Fiona said, her chin in the air with enough sass to make Grace smile and ease some of the tension from her shoulders.

"I think I'm going to have to cause some pretty big explosions to get this man's attention, let alone to change this ruling. How could something like this just happen? Don't they have to notify you before the land becomes available for lease? Can't we establish our rights, since we've lived here continuously for years? I just don't understand any of this," Grace said, reaching up to braid her long hair. It was an unconscious habit, something many of the women in her family did when they were agitated.

"I can't say. The land was given to me and I haven't much thought about it since, to be completely honest. However, I suspect you'll find a way to make this right. Don't you worry, Gracie. This cottage was standing long before Dylan set foot on this land and it will stand long after. You're smart enough and strong enough to figure this out," Fiona said, beaming at Grace over the table.

"I haven't heard from my parents. I know they said they'd have limited access to email on this cruise, but I thought I'd have more contact with them. Should I make an emergency call to the ship?"

"I believe the universe has a timing for things and a way of sorting things out. Perhaps they were meant to be unavailable, solely for the reason that this isn't their hurdle to face. It's yours. Tell me, and look deep inside, is this your problem or theirs?"

Grace paused. It wasn't that she was used to running to her parents to solve her problems; oh no, she was far too independent for that. It was more that she was used to including them in every aspect of her life. It was weird to not share something so large with them.

"It's my problem to solve. And solve it I will. It's just weird not to tell Mum about any of this," Grace acknowledged.

"Sometimes love needs space to blossom without parental judgment or insight weighing heavy upon it. It gives you freedom to think about what you want out of your relationship and not what they want or expect for you," Fiona observed.

Grace's jaw dropped. "This isn't... I'm not talking about love. I'm talking about being evicted from this land and Dylan" – her voice softened at his name – "wanting to build on the cove and bulldoze your cottage."

"And why aren't you talking about love? This is the man you've dreamed about for ages. What did he tell you in the last dream? Where you asked him what he wanted you to learn?"

"He told me he's here," Grace said, her voice cracking as she remembered. "He said he's right here."

"And so he is. You don't think you'll be pulling the wool over my eyes on this one, do you? This is your great love. What do you plan to do about it?" Fiona folded her arms across her chest.

"I... I have absolutely no idea," Grace admitted, surprised to find that it was true. She hated not having an answer for the problems at hand, and this particular problem had just grown thorns, wrapped brambles around her heart, and threatened to suffocate her.

"Well, you'd better figure it out, because if you think for a second that Dylan is going to sit back and wait for you to make your next move, you'd be dead wrong. The man is a force of nature – no moss grows on him. While you sit here and pout, he's going to be building a counter-attack. I suggest you hit him on both levels – his heart and his business sense. But then, what do I know? I'm just an old woman ghost who pops into your kitchen once in a while."

With that, Fiona blinked away, presumably in a huff, leaving Grace glaring at the space she had just occupied.

"I'll remind you that I have several lifetimes under my

belt," Grace grumbled, getting up from the rocking chair. "I'm not scared of a battle."

Even so, Grace ducked her head when Fiona sent thunder rumbling over the cottage, and Rosie cast a worried look at the roof.

"Yeah, yeah, I hear you," Grace said, but blew a kiss into the air anyway. Fiona always knew how to make her point.

CHAPTER 12

*R*eluctant to leave her property, although she doubted Dylan would come swooping in to bulldoze her cottage, Grace spent the rest of the day researching land laws in Ireland. For what felt like the hundredth time, she found herself staring off into space, her mind hopelessly fixated on the way the wind had blown a tendril of hair across Dylan's forehead or the lazy confidence he displayed in the way he carried himself.

Disgusted with herself for feeling like a love-struck teenager when she'd only spoken a few words to the man, Grace pushed away from her laptop and moved to the cabinet that held a small selection of Ireland's finest whiskey offerings. She idly perused her choices but couldn't decide, so she picked a bottle at random and poured herself a glass before sliding into the rocking chair in front of the fire she'd lit hours ago. Rosie, stretched out on the floor, lifted her head to see if there was any chance of a biscuit before settling back into her snooze.

It was maddening, Grace thought as she contemplated

the flames and took a long pull from her whiskey glass. The layers between her lifetimes were blurring, and it was as if she were being pulled back into the moods and feelings of another woman, yet had to carry herself as a somewhat sane woman in this time. Which meant that she couldn't be aflutter for a man she'd just met – and one who was her adversary, at that. Not one person would believe or understand her feelings if she tried to explain them – well, perhaps her extended family would, with their magickal gifts, but for now Grace had to resign herself to the fact that Dylan Kelly was Public Enemy Number One in her world.

Which meant she'd need to conduct herself with care in his presence, and make sure he didn't wise up to her attraction. If he did, Grace was certain he'd use it against her. Dylan was a man who would use every tool available, and she was sure he wasn't above playing on a woman's interest if it got him what he wanted. And Grace refused to be one of the legions of women who seemed to hang on his arm in all his pictures.

She sighed and pinched her nose, taking another sip of whiskey and letting the heat of it warm her core. It hadn't taken her long to stray from looking up the boring laws of land rights and usage to scanning the society pages that seemed to love golden boy Dylan Kelly. If anyone asked her, Grace would lie through her teeth about the number of hours she'd spent Googling him, her nose wrinkled in a sneer at photo after photo of models and socialites draping his arms. The press loved him – from his philanthropic ways to his hardworking rags-to-riches story, to the way none of the women he dated ever had anything bad to say about him. Aside from the fact that he refused to commit, that is. It seemed he gently and kindly moved on from each woman, leaving them sighing after him, perpetually the one that got away. Whether it was his commitment to bachelorhood or his zest and enthusiasm for making money, Grace found herself distinctly annoyed by his life choices.

The Dillon she'd known had cared about the simple things in life – exploring the world, sharing stories, learning new trades. He hadn't been one for flash and extravagance. It would serve Grace well to remember that the man she'd met today had lived many lives since they had been together.

And so had she.

Grace downed her drink and whistled for Rosie to do her lock-up routine. Tamping down the fire, she readied herself for bed, exhausted after the upheaval of the day and the lack of sleep the night before. Maybe Fiona was right and she'd find the answer in her dreams that night. All she knew was that her emotions were stirred up, her mind was a tangled ball of confusion, and her heart felt like it wanted to jump out of her chest.

It wasn't long before she found herself back at the water's edge, her heart drawn irresistibly and inexplicably to where she knew her man waited. Except this time, it wasn't the lovely little strip of beach or the cottage they'd once shared together.

"There she is," Dylan laughed to her from where he stood, knee-deep in the water, a fishing line in his hand.

"You shouldn't fish in here," Grace said automatically, as she looked up at the almost perfect half-circle of cliffs that sheltered the enchanted waters of Grace's Cove – her cove.

"Food for my love. Love gives and love takes, sort of like the ebb and flow of the waves, no?" Dylan smiled easily at her as he threw the line once more and Grace drew closer, helpless not to be near him. He radiated confidence and love, smiling casually over his shoulder as he continued to cast his line for dinner.

"Love shouldn't take," Grace said, perching on a rock near him, unsure of where this dream was guiding her.

"Sure it should, Grace," Dylan said, using her name from this century, a sign that he didn't remember her from before. "If one person gives and gives love, but takes none in return, they'll end up an empty well. Don't you think love should flow like a circle between two people? Some days you may love them more than they love you, and vice versa, but isn't that the beauty of it? Together you are stronger than apart."

Grace considered his words, unsure of her footing here and in this time. Her heart knew this man before her, but her mind didn't. For all she knew, this could be some magickal life lesson being taught to her by Fiona or any other spirits who had a mind to meddle in her love life. Never stupid, Grace decided to proceed with caution.

"I suspect there is a yin-and-yang kind of flow to love, Dylan. You seem to be speaking from experience. Which of your women has taught you this love?"

Obviously Grace was still peeved over the women she'd seen in the online magazines earlier, or that little tidbit probably wouldn't have popped into her brain. Nonetheless, there it was.

"There's only one woman for me, Grace," Dylan said, his smile wide and his eyes patient.

"Excuse me if I'm struggling to believe that at the moment," Grace bit out, a sullen expression settling onto her face. "Seeing as how you don't even recognize me."

Dylan waded over to crouch down next to Grace. His fingers, wet with sea water, clutched her chin and forced her to tip her head up to meet his eyes. Her heart hammered in her chest – she so wanted to kiss this Dylan to see if he felt the same.

"My heart sees you," Dylan said, ever so softly, as he brought his palm to his chest.

Grace closed her eyes and turned away, blinking back the tears that suddenly threatened.

"But *you* don't," Grace whispered, turning once more to look at him when her eyes had cleared.

"Not yet. Have faith in me," Dylan said.

Grace woke to tears drying on her cheeks – this time not for the love she'd relived and lost, but for a new poignant ache that blossomed in her chest. With all the challenges set before them, Grace didn't think she could trust Dylan to see her – to really see her – for who she was to him.

She feared this might be one battle she'd end up losing.

CHAPTER 13

*T*ypically, Dylan was an early riser, as he often needed to field questions and answers from his offices in other countries. But this morning, he let his more-than-capable business managers attend to the details and instead he lingered in bed, his mind a morass of thoughts and emotions that stuck with him from his blurred dreams the night before. Most nights, after Dylan dropped into bed he slept an almost dreamless night through before waking early in the morning, refreshed and ready to conquer any new challenges that greeted him.

But, today, he lingered. The bed, a generous king-size, had soft cotton sheets and a handwoven quilt in muted greens and golds. As usual, he'd taken up the whole bed, spreading his arms wide and piling all the pillows behind his head. The view of the water from the wide window that lined the wall in front of the bed promised a rainy morning, and Dylan was in no mood to rush from his cozy spot.

He'd dreamt of her.

Dylan grimaced as he punched a pillow and propped himself further up in order to gaze out at where the water met the horizon, barely discernable as one grey line melded with another. Somehow he'd known she'd be in his dreams, but there was no reason for it. Other than the fact that it had been ages since he'd lain with a woman, and she was a rumpled delightful wonderland of curves and flushed skin... Dylan grimaced as lust surged through him. His dreams had been anything but chaste, and he'd woken up with a taste for her in his mouth.

Lust didn't bother Dylan. It was something that came naturally when a man had his eye on someone who pleased his senses. The problem was more with the words he had dreamed about whispering into her lips, promises of a love that transcended all time. Words that made him uncomfortable in the stark light of day, like someone had taken a chink out of the armor he wore around his heart. It was a feeling he didn't like, and one that he hoped could be tucked away. Because no matter how delightful a passing fancy with Grace would be, ultimately it would be unethical. He was her landlord, and it was best not to mix business with pleasure.

It was a policy that had served him well through the years. He'd only had to learn that lesson once, in his early days when he had tended bar at a local pub during university. It wasn't uncommon for his coworkers to have flings with each other – and every other uni student that passed through the door. He'd had his fair share of flings with the clientele, but had taken a particular shine to a new girl, Shelly, who had started working just after him. Young, naïve, and full of lust, he'd thought with the wrong head and dove into a heated three-week affair that had ended up poisoning his workplace when he'd called things off with Shelly. Dylan had found out that she didn't mind sharing herself with more than one lad at a time, which was something he'd not been particularly pleased with. When her other beaus had broken off with her as well, Shelly had flitted back to Dylan, hoping to catch his eye again. He'd refused her advances, and she'd gone on to make his working life hell. Ever since that time, he'd learned never to cross those lines, no matter the temptation at hand. It had made for smart business decisions, and ultimately he'd gained more friends and respect along the way for not crossing boundaries.

And a liaison with Ms. O'Brien, however tempting it might be, would most certainly muddy the water – water that he'd worked long and hard to clear his calendar for. Finally, he was able to work on a passion project after his heart – not one based on the financial outcome as well. The opportunity had come at a perfect time in his life, and Dylan was smart enough to not let a succulent rose of a woman cloud his head and pull his eyes from his goal.

He sighed, stretching his long body as his mind flitted over the more interesting aspects of his dream. If real life with Grace was anything like his dream, it was a damn shame he'd be passing her up. But Dylan was nothing if not focused when he had an end goal in mind. It was a trait of his that had won him the admiration of many who worked for him, along with his willingness to dive right into the trenches. Be it cleaning one of his boats or helping on a new construction build, Dylan was never too aloof to get his hands dirty.

Dylan let his mind wander over all the businesses he'd built since the time he'd bartended in college. University had been an easy study for him, and he'd double-loaded his classes to get in and out so he could take on the real world as quickly as he could. Luck had struck for Dylan early in the game, when a regular at the bar had invited him to come down to check out his boat one day. Never one to say no to a day on the water, Dylan had obliged and in a short time had struck up a friendship with the man. Soon the relationship had turned more into a mentorship, and he'd been taught the ways of shipbuilding, the ins and outs of running a business, and what to look for when hiring employees. Spying a keen eye for business and an aptitude to excel, his mentor had bankrolled Dylan's first boat, and the rest, as they say, was history.

Dylan had named his first boat *The Pirate Queen*, much to the delight of his investor. In five years' time, he'd tripled his boat inventory, and had set up daily tours and shipping routes all over Ireland. In ten years' time, he'd expanded his business into worldwide enterprises. Dylan never stopped learning, and he always loved a challenge. But in the last year or two, things had grown stagnant for him. It had only been when he'd decided one day to sail down the coast of Ireland for a few weeks, taking his favorite boat, *The Pirate Queen*, and a few of his best mates with him, that he'd discovered something that called to his heart once more.

They'd had great craic, with Liam at the helm – swinging the boat into various ports along the coast, telling tall tales in little harbor towns, meeting pretty girls they'd slip away from at dawn, all the while taking a much-needed respite from the demands of running a worldwide company. But when they'd worked their way down the coast and stumbled upon the little village of Grace's Cove, Dylan had stood up and taken notice.

It had felt like coming home.

Colorful houses clustered on the green hills rising up from the water, like brightly colored ornaments on a Christmas tree. Single-lane roads wove here and there, the cars not paying too much mind as to which way to travel, only giving a casual beep and wave to go ahead when meeting one another on the lane. Fishing boats huddled each night at the harbor, and the delicious scents of the fresh catch grilling at quaint restaurants wafted through the air. Perhaps it was no less and no more pretty than any other harbor town he'd docked *The Pirate Queen* at, but Dylan fell instantly and head over heels in love with Grace's Cove.

Since that time, Dylan had been determined to find a way to come back. At first, Liam had suggested he just buy a holiday home in the village and visit a few weeks a year. But that hadn't been enough for Dylan. He needed to make a mark – to *do something* here – and the thought of coming back to Grace's Cove had been like an itch between his shoulders that he couldn't reach, until he'd upped and said no to any new projects and had come to the village to see his dream through. His managers had all looked shocked when he'd personally given them raises, more responsibilities, and the authority to make decisions without him having to sign off on every document. Dylan trusted implicitly the people he'd brought into his company, and they'd more than proven themselves over the years.

So here he was – alone in this bed; dreaming of a witchy-eyed woman with mermaid hair, who he was more than certain had some kind of magick readily at her disposal; with a stalled construction project, no pressing deadlines on any of his businesses, and a slew of unanswered questions about just what kind of magick he was actually dealing with at the cove.

His lips quirked as he thought about his mother and how delighted she would be if she knew he was taking magick seriously. She'd always had a fanciful side to her, reading to Dylan the myths of mermaids or the selkies who haunted the waters. Catherine loved nothing more than to find stone circles, read about pagan rituals, and set up crystals to shoo fairies from her gardens. She'd promised Dylan that one day, as he rode his boat over the waters, he'd see something that he wouldn't be able to explain away with all his pragmatic logic and business sense. Ever the sailor, Dylan had indulged his mother in her stories – and sure, there was a time or two while at sea that he might – *might* – have glimpsed something on the horizon that he couldn't explain. Catherine liked to insist it was the mermaids. Dylan liked to insist she'd had one too many whiskies before bed each night.

Glancing at the phone that buzzed by his side, Dylan's lips curved into a smile.

"Mum, you'll never guess. I think I've finally seen a mermaid."

Her squeal of delight was enough to cheer him up, and

soon he'd forgotten the unsettling dreams of the night before and was ready to get on with his day.

With the first stop being to investigate the supposed 'enchanted waters' of this cove that he'd heard so much about over dinner the night before.

CHAPTER 14

Grace had started her morning with a quick visit to Martin who, to her delight, had not only spent much of the previous day writing and filing the injunction she'd requested, but had also, it seemed, made moves where his secretary Anne was concerned.

He had just quietly informed Grace of a few things she might be able to add to her strategy, should it become necessary.

"So you're saying I can sue him?" Grace asked, arms crossed over her chest. In a nod to the misty weather, she'd worn her favorite hunter green canvas field jacket, slim denim pants tucked into Wellies, and a tartan scarf in cheerful shades of red and blue wound around her neck. Her hair, always moody in the damp weather, was left to tumble down her back, as subduing it would have taken more energy than Grace had been willing to expend that morning.

"You don't have to sue him," Martin had said, steepling his hands over the notepad on his desk. "However, should the injunction not do the trick – and you do know how big corporations like to push the little guys around – you can sue him for not publicly notifying you of his purchase. Technically, you should have had sufficient notice in order to either extend the lease yourself, or to be offered the fair market value of the property. I'd say unless some paperwork got lost in the mail, he didn't bother to notify you. And the law requires at least several attempts at notification – you can't just mail a postcard and consider the matter sorted."

Martin had looked particularly pleased with his work, and even more so when Grace had rounded the desk to give him a smacking kiss on the cheek before sailing out to the front office, a happy Rosie at her heels.

"You look nice today, Anne," Grace had said to the assistant, who wore a cheerful red polka-dotted blouse tucked into trim black slacks.

"Thank you, Grace," Anne had said demurely, then winked at a grinning Grace as she left the office.

Grace felt much better knowing she had a way out, or at the very least some ammunition to fight this battle. As for matters of the heart, that was another thing entirely. For now, she'd deal with one thing at a time. Securing her home, her cove, and her livelihood came first. Love – well, it would have to just wait.

She found herself humming on the drive home along the cliffs. It had been a considerably productive morning, from what she'd learned at the solicitor's office to picking up various items from the garden shop and market that she needed for a few different tinctures she was experimenting with. Usually Grace grew, cultivated, and charmed most of her own ingredients, but sometimes the bit players in her concoctions didn't need that level of attention. As her chef friend had once told her, why make a béchamel sauce from scratch when you can just pour it from the bottle into the recipe?

When her truck crested the final hill that wound its way toward the cove and her cottage, Grace's good mood vanished.

"The nerve of that man," Grace hissed, and Rosie straightened at Grace's tone.

Grace parked her truck next to Dylan's, refusing to slam on the brakes or drive angrily – mainly because Rosie was in the car. Grace would never forgive herself if she sent her dog flying into the windshield because she had driven carelessly when her temper kicked up. Plus, a cooler head always prevailed, she reminded herself and whistled for Rosie to join her as she strode across the damp grass to the cove.

Rosie, knowing exactly where they were headed, bolted ahead down the path that led to the entrance to the cove. Switch-backing down the cliff walls like a big Z, the path led to a pristine sand beach untouched by man, protected by the cliff walls and the magick Grace had infused it with so many centuries ago. Blood magick – the serious kind, for which she'd given her life – had protected her resting place, enchanted the waters found here, and given those born of her blood extra magickal gifts to aid them in their lives. It had been a sacrifice, and one well worth making. Grace had known the disease she carried had no cure, and the end had been near. She'd never been prouder of herself, or her daughter, than that night so many ages ago on the beach that spread below her now.

Shaking her head to clear the memory, Grace started down the path, muttering the whole time about idiot men meddling in things they had no knowledge of. She hoped Dylan had done enough research to know not to enter the cove on his own – any local would have warned him away, not to mention the signs that were posted about trespassing and dangerous undertows.

As Grace reached the beach, she looked up at Rosie's sharp bark and swore loudly as her stomach dropped. Rosie paced in circles around a body, prone on the beach, and whined in concern.

Breaking into a run, Grace could only pray that, all these years later, her own magick wouldn't turn against her.

CHAPTER 15

"Of all the damn fool things," Grace cursed as she dropped to her knees at Dylan's head. She ran her fingers over his neck to find a pulse. Finding him alive but knocked out, Grace let out a stream of curses that would have made a sailor blush.

At the very least, they were enough to bring one very cranky sailor awake.

"What… what happened?" Dylan asked, blinking up at Grace, his sunny blue eyes clouded by confusion as his gaze landed on hers. "Mermaid."

"What?" Grace asked, looking behind her.

"You. Mermaid," Dylan said, reaching up to toy with the ends of the hair that tumbled over her shoulder. "Sunset hair and witchy eyes. Mermaid."

"What I am is a very angry woman," Grace said, unceremoniously running her hands over his body, looking with her mind's eye for any bumps, internal bleeding, or broken bones. Only when she threaded her hands through his thick blond hair did she find the bump. Pulling a hand away and finding it covered with blood, she swore once more.

"Mermaid with a dirty mouth. Sexy," Dylan mused, his smile the loopy grin of someone still not totally coherent.

"That's me, sexy as can be. Hold still, would you?" Grace asked when he continued to try and run his hands through her hair. Reaching up, she placed both hands on his head and, using an age-old technique that had been passed down through her family, she centered her mind and healed him on the spot. When a boulder crashed further down the beach, Dylan tore his gaze away from hers to look.

Grace pulled back and waited, calming herself as she always needed to do after a healing, before quietly meeting Dylan's watchful gaze.

"What did you just do?" Dylan asked.

"Just put a bit of salve on your wounds," Grace said, lying easily about her gift and holding up a jar she kept tucked away in her purse. "Old pagan remedy. You'll be right as rain soon enough."

She didn't like the way he was eyeing her so she stood, hands on her hips, and stared down at him.

"Are you a complete idiot then?" Grace asked, finally letting the fury she'd been holding in check bubble to the surface.

Dylan's expression flashed from contemplative to mutinous, and Grace understood instantly that she'd offended his male pride. Too bad she didn't care about male egos and all the soothing gestures women claimed they needed to make. The man had been an idiot. The fact was indisputable.

"Sure and that's not typically a word applied to me," Dylan said, leaping to his feet so that he wasn't lying in the sand at a disadvantage anymore. Grace glanced over him, from the sand stuck to his sodden jeans to the few drops of blood that marred his grey wool jacket. She shook her head, purposely letting a look of disgust settle on her face as her eyes roamed over him.

"I know what I'm looking at, don't I? And that's an idiot of a man. One who ignores the signs about trespassing on private land. One who ignores the signs about the dangerous undertow of this beach. One who has most likely ignored the warnings of the locals about coming here. And don't try and tell me that none of the locals warned you. Sure and that's hard to believe. We've lost people over the years because of their stupidity. You could've been next." With that, Grace turned on her heel and stormed down the beach for the path. To hell with him, she thought. There was no way she could love a man that harebrained – that stubborn – as to willingly put his life in danger out of mere curiosity.

"Hold up," Dylan said, grabbing Grace's arm. She whirled, fist up, ready to sock him one if he tried anything silly. Immediately understanding he was being rough with her, Dylan swore and took his hands from her, instead tucking them in his pockets.

"Hands off, Kelly," Grace said, narrowing her eyes at him and refusing to acknowledge that her heart wanted to insist that no, indeed, she very much wanted him to be hands on.

"I'm sorry, I shouldn't have grabbed you that way. Especially after you helped me. I... I don't really know what happened. I wasn't even trying to go in the water. I just wanted a better look at the beach that everyone talks about. I..." Dylan shrugged. Confusion crossed his handsome features as he looked back over the beach.

"There's a strong undertow here. Sometimes the waves are stronger than expected and reach much higher than people on the beach would think. I suspect a rogue wave smacked you and you knocked your head on a rock. Luckily, I was on my way home and saw your truck, or who knows how long you would have been down there," Grace said. "Next time... actually, never mind; there will *be* no next time. You're not allowed on my property. Next time I'll leave you to drown, if you insist on being so stupid."

"I'm getting pretty annoyed with the number of times you're calling my intelligence into question, Grace," Dylan said, stepping closer so that he towered over her. Grace could read the instant when his energy changed from anger to a confusion of lust and attraction. Reaching out, he danced his fingertips over the tail ends of her hair.

"That's Ms. O'Brien to you. And I call it as I see it. You're welcome to prove me wrong, but thus far, I'm not impressed," Grace said. So saying, she turned on her heel and whistled for Rosie, beginning the climb up the cliff walls – leaving behind her a very angry, very frustrated, and very aroused male.

"I accept that challenge, Ms. O'Brien," Dylan called after her.

And damn it, but his words did put a smile on her face.

CHAPTER 16

"So you went to the cove alone," Liam said, shaking his shaggy head at Dylan as he sipped his Guinness. They were at a cozy little fisherman's shack of a restaurant whose outward appearance belied the mouthwatering scents wafting from the kitchen, tucked behind the bar they now sat at. They'd been told an hour wait for dinner, and had been lucky enough to snag two stools at the small bar. Dylan was finally relaxing enough to recount the day he'd had.

"Aye, that I did. I wanted to see what all the fuss was about." Dylan shrugged, unable to explain the pull to the cove he felt. Or perhaps it had been the pull to see Grace again, he mused, having had difficulty putting her out of his mind since she'd stormed away from him earlier today. He'd be lying if he said he didn't enjoy the flash of fire in her eyes, the toss of her hair as she stormed away, or the way her tight denim pants hugged a bum that would make most men's mouths water. She was a dangerous package – and one he'd do well to stay far away from.

"How'd that work out for you?" Liam asked, amusement flashing over his face.

"About as well as could be expected," Dylan admitted, and Liam chuckled.

"From what I hear, you have to do some sort of ritual to even step onto the beach. And it isn't something that's widely shared – some sort of decision was made years ago where the locals banded together as one to keep people from entering the water there."

"I'd say that was a smart move on their part," Dylan said, draining his gin and tonic and gesturing to the bartender for one more. He'd been on edge all day since leaving the cove.

"Did something happen?"

"You could say that," Dylan said, rolling the tension from his shoulders. He'd had no pain since the incident, and hardly a lump on his head. Certainly not anything large enough to warrant him being knocked unconscious. Some salve Grace had, he mused.

"And the plot thickens," Liam said, winking at the girl who came to serve them their drinks and making her smile back.

"Everything seemed normal," Dylan grumbled. "Until it wasn't. It's stunning down there. The cliff walls rise so high around you, enclosing you in this almost complete circle. It's quiet too – nothing but the waves lapping the shore and a few birds swooping by. No wonder the locals don't want tourists going there. It's a pristine slice of paradise."

"It's certainly stunning from above," Liam agreed.

"So there I am, enjoying the beauty, just strolling along

and taking it all in – trying to get a feel for the energy there," Dylan said.

"Ah, himself isn't immune to feeling for magick," Liam mused.

"Himself is enough of a sailor to know there are things that can't be explained," Dylan agreed.

"Yet you try to dismiss the horns honking and the car doors crashing open as a gust of wind." Liam chuckled to himself at that.

"It's a possibility," Dylan grumbled, squeezing a lime into his drink.

"A small one," Liam said, "but I digress. So you're having yourself a lovely little wander on this magickal beach you've been warned away from, and then what?"

"And then… I don't know. Next thing I know I'm opening my eyes to a woman with a nice turn of phrase when it comes to cusswords, fiery hair, and a temper to match," Dylan said.

"Ms. O'Brien. She's a fine woman," Liam decided, raising a Guinness in a silent toast to Grace.

"Even while she was letting me know just what a complete and total idiot she thought I was, she was also running her hands all over my body –"

"Mmm, I like where this is going. Tell me more," Liam said, a delighted grin flashing on his face.

"She was looking for injuries, not to jump me," Dylan sighed.

"More's the pity," Liam said, and they both drank silently to that thought.

"I was still quite dazed, and convinced she was a mermaid, when she found a wound at the back of my head. One that was quite bloody, mind you, judging by the blood that washed out in the shower later. She ran her hands over the wound, and then..." Dylan shrugged, unsure how to describe what he'd felt. He'd still been quite dazed.

"And then what?" Liam asked, raising an eyebrow at Dylan in question.

"It felt like some sort of cool brush of air... soothing, ye know? When I next touched my head, the wound was but a little lump. Certainly not enough to knock me unconscious, nor to bleed to the extent it had," Dylan said, meeting Liam's eyes. "You know I'm capable of taking some strong hits to the head."

"Aye, that I do. There was that one night in Glasgow..." Liam pursed his lips in fond memory of one of their more debauchery-driven evenings, which had landed both of them with sore knuckles and Dylan with an eye swollen shut.

"That there was," Dylan said, and then gestured to the back of his head. "Feel."

Liam reached over and patted Dylan's head, and found nothing of interest. Pulling his hand back, he leveled a look at Dylan.

"No bump."

"Indeed, no bump. Now, shouldn't there be a bump on me own head if I was hit hard enough to bleed and knock myself unconscious?" Dylan asked.

"She healed you."

"Aye. She claims she just put some pagan salve on my head and that I'd feel no pain, but I'm not so certain. Frankly, I was so intoxicated with thinking she was a mermaid that it took a moment for my brain to catch up to reality."

"I can see her being a mermaid. She'd charm many a sailor, that's for damn sure," Liam said agreeably.

"I barely had time to be charmed before she cussed me out once more, called me an idiot in several different ways, and stormed off down the path with her dog at her side. It was like being ravaged by a tornado of beauty."

Liam brought his fingers to his pursed lips and kissed them.

"My kind of woman. You know the ones who don't give their opinions on anything will ultimately end up boring you to death," Liam pointed out.

"I'm not interested in a relationship with Grace," Dylan said patiently, for his friend liked to indulge in as many romances as possible and always looked for love wherever he could find it.

"You may not be interested in one, but I suspect one's found you nonetheless," Liam said, his voice decidedly cheerful at the thought.

"Not even close. Remember, I'm her landlord and I'm evicting her. I won't cross those lines," Dylan said, then looked up when a man approached them, his face set in grim lines.

"Um, excuse me, gentlemen. My name is Daniel and I'm the manager of the restaurant. I'm very sorry, but we'll be unable to serve you dinner this evening." Daniel wrung his hands, clearly unhappy at having to deliver such news.

"Is that so?" Dylan leaned back and smiled at the man. "Run out of fresh catch of the day?"

"Oh, no, sir. We never run out," Daniel said, glancing between Liam and Dylan, concern etched on his features.

"Then what seems to be the problem, my good man?" Liam asked, his tone lazy, though his eyes had gone hard.

"I'm not sure how best to state this…" Daniel said, and Dylan had a suspicion that he knew what was about to come.

"Best to be out with it quickly then," he said.

"The owner of this restaurant is Grace O'Brien's father. We've received notice that we're not to be serving you or your crew any meals or refreshments. I do apologize or I wouldn't have even sat you at the bar. It's only just come to my attention who you are."

"And who are we?" Dylan asked.

"Why, you're the corporation that's trying to bulldoze Grace's cottage and build condos on her land. That simply won't do. My deepest apologies, but I do have to ask you to leave now," Daniel said, his tone stern as voices lowered in the restaurant to watch the scene.

"Certainly, I understand," Dylan said, and slipped some bills from his wallet to cover the cost of the drinks. They walked from the now near-silent restaurant, Liam cheekily grinning back at the cute waitress, and in moments were back in the cool night air.

"Daddy's got connections," Liam observed.

"Daddy's famous for his restaurants and fishing charters all over Ireland," Dylan mused, rocking back on his heels as he tucked his hands in his pockets. "I've met him and quite like him. But I can understand why he issued the order he did. I'd do the same."

"Why didn't you tell him that you aren't building condos?" Liam asked.

"Let them think what they want. I suspect the element of surprise will serve me well at some point here."

"Playing the long game?" Liam asked as they turned to find another place for a warm meal.

"Aye, playing the long game."

CHAPTER 17

he knock at her door just past the first blush of dawn had Rosie going ballistic and Grace cursing as she wrapped a towel around her and bolted for the door. Her brain still foggy from a poor night's sleep, Grace opened the door without preamble. She assumed it to be one of her family, because no one with any sense in their head would call upon someone at this hour.

"Ah, good, you're awake," Dylan said, smiling at her from behind a basket he held in front of him.

Grace glared at him, feeling out of sorts, for she hadn't had her tea yet and the man had caught her half-dressed and dripping wet. With her hair streaming down her back and making a small pool of water on the floor, Grace had to decide whether to go put on clothes or order Dylan on his way.

"Barely. Are you lost then?" Grace said, leaning against the frame of the door and deciding it was best to not invite the man inside.

"Some may think that. But I'm beginning to feel right

at home," Dylan said, flashing her a slow smile as his eyes trailed over her shoulders, which were flushed pink from the heat of the shower.

"Cool it with the come-hither smoldering stares, okay, Kelly? You're Public Enemy Number One and are not welcome here," Grace said, lifting her chin into the air.

"I understand that. But I've brought a peace offering of sorts." Dylan's gaze slid past Grace to her stove. "And I see you haven't put tea on. Why don't I put it on for you while you get dressed and you can open your gift?" Neatly taking control of the situation, Dylan slipped past an astonished Grace and set his basket on the table, bending once to pat an ecstatic Rosie – the traitor – before he moved to the rack that held the tea mugs. Grace didn't want to think about how good he looked in her kitchen, and retreated quickly into her bedroom. It seemed like the man planned to settle in for a wee visit, and she'd only be uncomfortable if she stood there holding a towel around her dripping wet body for the entire time. Briefly, she entertained shooing him off with magick, but despite herself, she wanted to see what was in the basket he'd brought.

Hastily wrapping her hair in a towel, Grace pulled on soft leggings and an oversized sweatshirt before spending a brief moment wringing as much of the water from her hair as she could. Letting the mass of it stream down her back, she pulled on thick cottage socks and padded silently to the door, easing it open to watch as Dylan neatly prepared the tea at the counter, while seemingly having a discussion with her dog.

"I'm certain it would be frowned upon to give you a piece of these scones. But I suspect there's a cookie jar around here somewhere for you," Dylan said. Upon hearing the word 'cookie,' Rosie dashed to sit in front of the jar. It annoyed Grace how at home Dylan had made himself in her cottage – a cottage that he wanted to force her out of, she reminded herself. His presence here felt larger than life, the juxtaposition of his size and strength against the dainty lace curtains and the low ceilings of the cottage seeming to highlight his stark masculinity. Breathing out a small puff of air, Grace entered the room.

"Aye, there she is. Looking fresh as a daisy this morning," Dylan said, bringing tea to the table and placing the basket of scones she'd prepared earlier in the week in front of her. Grace narrowed her eyes at him serving her in her own home.

"Sit, drink your tea, then leave," Grace muttered, causing Dylan to throw his head back in laughter.

"You know, I'm beginning to like you, Grace."

"Whether you like me or not is irrelevant," Grace said, her eyes flashing a warning at him. *Liar, liar,* her heart whispered.

"Nevertheless, that's the way of it," Dylan said, sliding onto the bench seat across the table from her. The blue of the plaid shirt he wore highlighted his eyes, and Grace found herself itching to run her hands through the blond hair that had just begun to curl. To check his wounds, of course, she lectured herself. "I've brought you a gift."

"I'm not easily bought," Grace said, more sharply than she had intended – but hey, the man wanted her off what he considered to be his land.

Dylan's eyes flashed a warning, but Grace just raised an eyebrow at him and crossed her arms over her chest.

She didn't care for this cozy little scene he was trying to create, nor was she about to be his friend. Perhaps once he conceded that the land belonged to her and her family, Grace would take the time to examine her attraction to him more closely.

"As a thank you," Dylan said, his tone mild, but Grace recognized the steel beneath the tone.

"No thank you is necessary. I'm not sure what it's like where you're from, but we're not ones to leave an injured man untended in these parts," Grace shrugged, still refusing to touch the basket in front of her.

"Strange; it doesn't feel to me like I was all that injured," Dylan said, leaning back and letting his eyes travel over the shelves upon shelves of jars that lined the wall behind Grace's head. "That's some salve you have there."

"That it is. We're healers in these parts. In the old ways," Grace said, not elaborating further.

"Seems to work well for you," Dylan nodded.

"That it does. So if it's a gift of thanks you're bringing, I'll be opening it. But don't be surprised if it gets donated or shared with others. I may not want your bad energy in the house," Grace said, knowing her words bordered on mean, but not really caring all that much.

"Do you think I have bad energy?" Dylan said, unoffended by her words, his bright blue eyes studying her over the rim of his tea cup.

"I think you're a pragmatic businessman who is used to getting, and determined to get, his own way. Now, I'm certainly not one to judge a man for wanting to further his station in life and build something that matters for himself, but the way in which he achieves such things matters. To my mind, you've gone about this entire situation in a very bad way. Which, in turn, brings bad energy into this space." Grace pulled at the ribbon that held the basket handles together, keeping the tone of her voice light.

"Perhaps I have," Dylan conceded, gripping his hand around the mug as he stared off into space. "Will you let me make it up to you?"

Her heart leaped in her chest at the thought – and what it could mean crashed through her. Being so near to him – yet unable to touch him, hold him, sing out her love for him – was wearing on her. Having to constantly hold her shield up and channel her inner pirate warrior queen was achingly difficult around Dylan.

"I don't know yet," Grace said.

"Let's start with the gift then," Dylan said, nudging the basket closer to her.

Grace had always loved gifts, and she tried her best to keep her expression reserved as she opened the lid on the basket.

"Ah, sure and that's a fine bottle of whiskey then," Grace said, pulling out a bottle of 15 Year Tyrconnell. Grace noted that he'd spent enough on a bottle to make it a nice gift while not being showy or ostentatious, though she was certain the man could probably buy the whole distillery if he wanted.

"Aye. I figured a woman who could curse as colorfully as you must have sailor's blood somewhere in her veins. As such, whiskey seemed an appropriate gift," Dylan said, and despite herself, Grace smiled at him.

"Sure and I wouldn't be a good Irish lass if I didn't

enjoy a pour of whiskey or putting a man in his place every now and again," Grace said, looking up at Dylan cheekily.

"Duly noted," Dylan said, chuckling softly and nodding for her to continue.

"A book?"

"I'm told it's quite rare," Dylan said, shrugging as Grace ran her hands over the aged leather and turned it to read the title.

"*The Healings of the Earth: Wild Women Recipes and Remedies*," Grace read, surprised and delighted with his choice. Flipping through the pages, she immediately saw several recipes and concoctions she'd be interested in testing out. Holding it up in the air, she gave Dylan her first genuine smile. "This is really lovely. I'll actually use this. Thank you."

"Ah, I wondered if I would ever see it," Dylan said, his eyes crinkling at the corners as he looked at her.

"See what?"

"A genuine smile on your face. It's a shame you don't use it more often. While you're a knockout package as you are, your smile is like the sun."

Charmed despite herself, Grace smiled at him once more, this time infusing some sass into it.

"Had I known it would take but a genuine smile for you to be nice to me, I would have used it sooner."

"Have I not been nice to you then?" Dylan said, his brows drawn in confusion.

Grace threw back her head and laughed, long and loud, so that Rosie bounced over to see what all the fun was about.

"Threatening to throw me off my land and tear down a cottage that has been in my family for generations isn't particularly kind, no," Grace said, amused with him.

"I understand it's not ideal," Dylan conceded, making Grace laugh again. "But I don't think I've been mean to you."

"No, you haven't been mean. Maddeningly calm, stubborn, and patronizing all at once. I'm sure you're a bulldog in the boardroom," Grace laughed, and then squinted at the basket. "Is that a rubber bone?"

"Yes! It's for Rosie," Dylan said, pulling the red rubber bone out of the basket and brandishing it in front of him. "See the slits in the side? You can put biscuits in there and she has to work them out. It's kind of a puzzle."

He'd brought a puzzle for her dog. Grace stared at him, utterly charmed, as he held the bone out for Rosie to sniff and then, comfortable in this space, moved to the counter and dug a few biscuits out. Rosie danced at his feet, anxious for treats, and then cocking her head when he offered her the bone again.

"See?" Dylan said, letting her sniff the toy. "They're in there. You just have to work on getting them out." Seeming to understand his words, Rosie nipped the bone from his hand and moved to her bed by the fireplace, completely absorbed in her new game.

"She'll love that," Grace said. "So, once again, I'll thank you."

"Two thank yous, a smile, and a laugh – I'll take that as a sign of progress," Dylan said, leaning against the wall by the door and nodding to her basket. "There's more."

"More?" Grace shook her head and dug in the basket to pull out… socks. "Socks?"

"They reminded me of you," Dylan said, a shy smile on his face. Grace looked at him in confusion before unrolling the socks to see scales in a rainbow of colors that rioted together to form the shape of fins.

"What are these?"

"Mermaid socks," Dylan said, delighted with himself. "I was convinced you were a mermaid yesterday. I saw these and thought of you. Sunset hair and witchy eyes."

"I'm no mermaid," Grace said, though a part of her secretly delighted in the thought.

"What are you then, Grace?" Dylan asked, leveling his gaze on her. A shiver raced over her skin as she felt the shift in energy in the room.

"Why, don't you know, Dylan? I'm a pirate queen, of course." Grace tossed the words away with a cheeky smile, wanting to defuse the tension while also avoiding the real question he was trying to ask her. She wasn't yet ready to talk about her magick with him.

"What did you say?" Dylan snapped, and Grace drew back as the color seemed to seep from his face.

"I said I'm a pirate queen," Grace said, wondering what had caused the change in his demeanor. Was he finally remembering who she was? Hope blossomed in her chest and she waited, a small smile hovering on her lips. *I'm right here*, her heart whispered.

Dylan shook his head, as if to clear his thoughts, and whatever he'd been about to say was gone.

"I have to go, Grace. Will you let me buy you a drink?"

Grace leveled a look at him and then held up the bottle of whiskey. "You already have."

"Then dinner? I'd like to make it up to you. Perhaps we can work together."

"I doubt that, as our goals are too far apart. But I'll think about it," Grace said, her eyes tracing over the nice gifts he'd brought to her.

"I'll be at the pub this evening. I'll wait for you."

Dylan didn't wait for her answer. Instead he left her with a pile of gifts, a mind full of questions, and a heart that dared to hope.

CHAPTER 18

*H*e'd had to get out of the cottage.

Dylan stopped his truck by the cove. Ignoring the light mist that sent particles of water through the air, he strode to the edge of the cliff and looked down at the waters that caressed the sand far below him.

Never in his life had his resolve been tested so seriously. When Grace had opened the door wrapped in nothing but a towel, her hair streaming behind her, her skin flushed from the shower, it was like having his knees kicked out from under him. Dylan had wanted nothing more than to lean in and press a kiss to the tender skin at her shoulder blade, to run his hands over the curves that the seriously small towel did little to hide, and to pick her up and carry her back to the bedroom. Everything in his body had screamed at him to do so, and it had only been his steely business resolve that had kept him from what he was certain would have been a huge mistake.

When she'd come out of her bedroom, having given him some time to cool off, she'd looked just as delectable in her oversized sweatshirt, loose hair, and makeup-free face. Her eyes, huge pools of misty sea blue, dominated her face and he wondered if she knew that they flitted between colors when her mood changed.

He hadn't come here for romance, though Liam liked to remind him that there was always time for that. Unfortunately, even Liam wouldn't be able to support Dylan if he seduced Grace and then kicked her out of her cottage. It would be indefensible.

"Pirate queen," Dylan hissed from between his teeth as he stared at the moody waters far below him. He wondered what kind of joke she was playing, or what magick she was wielding. Surely she'd said that to toy with his head. There had to be some way Grace had found out the name of his first and favorite boat. But *The Pirate Queen* was currently making her way along the coast of Ireland, her hold full of supplies, and nobody in Grace's Cove had seen her docked at the village.

Unless Grace had seen the boat when he had last sailed here. That was it, Dylan decided, turning his back on the cove and making his way through what was beginning to be a full-on downpour. Grace wasn't above using trickery to get her way, Dylan thought, and he had to admit he admired her for it.

If this were a chess match, he'd be hard-pressed to say who the victor would be. As a man who rarely liked to lose, Dylan would still put his money on himself. So long as Grace kept her smile to herself.

That alone could bring a stronger man than he to his knees.

CHAPTER 19

"*J*'m not going to the pub to see him," Grace said to Rosie. The dog gave her a side-eye, and then sauntered over to pick up her new bone in her mouth. Coming back to where Grace stood in front of her closet, the dog dropped the bone at her feet.

"I don't care what you say. I'm going to see Cait. She's worried about me," Grace insisted as she pushed through her hangers in the small closet in her room.

"Rosie's not buying it, and neither am I." Fiona's voice jarred Grace into almost rapping her head on the door of the closet. Turning to glare at her over her shoulder, Grace raised her lip in a snarl.

"Don't look at me like that. You know I'm right," Fiona said, sitting on Grace's bed with cheerful smile on her face.

"I'm looking at you because you always pick these inopportune times to pop in and say hello. I swear, it's almost like you enjoy scaring people." Grace slitted her eyes at Fiona. "You do, don't you? Oh my goddess, you like haunting people."

"Well, I would never purposely haunt someone. But if I startle someone on occasion, I can't help but find it a tad amusing, can I?" Fiona fussed, her nose in the air.

"Are you telling me you like to play pranks on people now that you're a ghost?" Grace demanded, her hands on her hips.

"I wouldn't say pranks. Just… moments to lighten the mood is all," Fiona sniffed.

"Lighten the mood, she says. What's fun for you is probably terrifying for whomever you're pranking." Grace shook her head and turned back to her wardrobe.

"I like the red blouse," Fiona said.

"This one?" Grace asked, pulling out a silky red blouse that skimmed her curves in all the right places.

"Yes. With your dark denim pants. And those pretty silver dangles Aislinn got for you from Greece."

"Oh, those are great earrings," Grace agreed, and soon enough she was dressed, standing before the mirror to pay attention to her makeup.

"Nothing too fussy now. And leave your mouth plain. Men like to look at a mouth they can kiss," Fiona instructed, and Grace slanted a glance at her.

"There will be no kissing. And I'll wear whatever makeup brings me joy or makes me happy – not to impress or please a man. Any man. Got it?"

"I've always liked your spunk, Gracie," Fiona said.

Grace smiled at her. "And I yours."

"So he brought you gifts, did he?"

"Aye, he did. Good ones, too. Rosie's chewing on one

of them," Grace said, nodding to where Rosie nosed the bone around the room.

"Smart man to think of the dog. And sweet, at that," Fiona noted.

"Perhaps, but I still don't see a way around any of this. He wants the land. I will fight for this land. He can be sweet on me all he wants – or I on him – but unless he backs down and walks away from this project, we've no future together. I have to accept that," Grace said, holding up a hand to stop Fiona from speaking. "I understand that you believe him to be my great love. But I'm also a realist and an adult. I have to accept the fact that if the man doesn't change his mind, there will be no way I can be with him. It would be impossible for me to forgive him if he kicked me off my land and tore this cottage down. You do understand that, don't you?"

"I do," Fiona said, her voice soft, her eyes sad.

"Fiona, he doesn't remember me. I… I know we had something amazing in another lifetime. But he doesn't see me. And I don't think he will."

"He has his eyes on you. He sees you," Fiona said, glancing down to Rosie and her bone.

"He sees me, but he doesn't know me. There's too much between us now. I need to handle one problem at a time. For now, that's securing this land and protecting the cove, and my home."

"Then why are you making yourself all pretty to just go to the pub?" Fiona asked.

"Aren't you the one who taught me that a woman should use every weapon in her arsenal?" Grace parried, picking up her purse and tucking a few last things inside.

"So you do listen once in a while," Fiona murmured.

Grace chuckled. "I love you. Thank you for always being there for me. I'll keep you posted on what happens. Please try not to give me a heart attack the next time you visit – or anyone else, for that matter," Grace said, blowing Fiona a kiss and tucking more treats into Rosie's puzzle bone. She left the two to their own company – the dog and the ghost – and headed out to launch the next step in her battle strategy.

Make him grovel.

CHAPTER 20

*C*ait greeted Grace with a smile and a slow look up and down at her outfit.

"What was that look for?" Grace asked, coming to stand by the pass-through. The night looked like it was shaping up to be a busy one already.

"You look extra fancy tonight," Cait said.

Grace immediately felt foolish. "Is it too much? It's just a blouse and some earrings," she said, casting a look down at her outfit.

"In screaming come-hither red, that is," Cait said, winking at her before turning to shout down the bar, "Hold your horses, Sean McMadden, you'll get your pints when I'm giving them to you."

"Fiona made me wear it," Grace pouted, and Cait laughed.

"She's a matchmaker, that's for sure."

"What if I don't want a match to be made?" Grace asked, turning despite herself to scan the room. While families packed the booths to share an early supper, and several lads enjoyed their pints while watching the hurling match on the small screen on one wall, there was no sign of Dylan.

"Don't you?" Cait parried, smug as a pixie as she hummed her way through filling the orders that the sole waitress, Mary Shannon, called out to her.

"I have other things on my mind besides romance," Grace lied.

Cait just shook her head at Grace. "You can try that with someone else, but not with me. You're just lucky I'm too busy to get my claws into you or we'd be hashing this out right now," she said, her small body moving fast as she pulled pints and popped open beers with the ease of someone who had memorized every inch of her bar and the space around her.

"Do you need help? Where's Casey?" Typically, on Saturday nights, Cait had two women who took orders, pulled pints, and generally helped with the running of the pub. With two cooks in the kitchen, Gallagher's Pub usually hummed along like a well-oiled machine. On the few occasions it didn't, nobody paid much mind – that was the way of things in village life.

"She's running late this evening. Sick toddler, and Danny's not yet home from work," Cait said.

"I'll help," Grace said, and ducked under the pass-through, tucking her purse in a small cubby behind the counter. It wasn't her first time pulling pints for Cait, and certainly wouldn't be her last. At home here, she shot Mr. Murphy a smile that had the old man beaming back at her and holding his half-pint up for her to fill.

"Sure and I must have died and gone to heaven, for it's

an angel that I'm seeing," Mr. Murphy said, twinkling at her from his perch on the stool.

"Don't get it confused, my love, for I'm no angel," Grace said, but leaned over to press her lips to his papery cheek.

"Even better. I've always liked my women feisty," Mr. Murphy said, and Grace threw back her head and laughed.

It was at that moment that Dylan entered the pub, his gaze finding hers like a heat-seeking missile, and his eyes flashed as they locked with hers. Behind him, Liam paused and watched as his friend had a moment, before nudging him from his trance to walk forward.

"Now, Mr. Murphy, you'll need to watch out – for while I'm no angel, it's the devil himself who has just arrived," Grace said, knowing she was being just a bit bitchy, but not really caring. She was growing tired of constantly feeling longing for this man, anxiety about her home and her livelihood, and generally just being in an all-around mood about everything. Since the target of all her angst had just sailed through the door, she didn't see any reason not to serve him up on a platter to the locals.

"She wounds me, she does," Dylan said, his look shuttered as he held a hand to his heart and came to stand next to the old man on the stool.

"Women will do that, you know. All sugar and cream one day, and peppers and hot sauce the next. Keeps it interesting, that's for sure," Mr. Murphy said.

Dylan chuckled. "Can I buy you a pint then?"

"I wouldn't be saying no," Mr. Murphy said.

"Three pints of Guinness, please. And, of course, something for yourself," Dylan said, his smile challenging

Grace. He'd turned the situation neatly around and brought Mr. Murphy to his side. *Your move*, his expression seemed to be saying.

"I don't drink when I'm working," Grace said, just to be difficult, and moved down the bar to start the process of building the Guinness. She moved out of earshot of Dylan and spent some time catching up with the locals, flirting with a few regulars, before winding her way back to the men with their drinks.

"Any food tonight? Special is colcannon soup."

"I'll have a bowl, thanks," Liam said, smiling at her. "The name's Liam, by the way. We didn't get a chance to be formally introduced the other day."

The day when they'd stood on her cliffs with bulldozers, Grace thought and raised an eyebrow at him. He had the decency to flush before taking a long swallow of his drink.

"And this must be the DK of DK Enterprises that I've heard so much chatter about in here," Cait said, coming to stand by Grace's side.

"Aye, that's myself, Dylan Kelly, and my project manager, Liam Mulder," Dylan said. Cait took his proffered hand, coolly assessing him before releasing it and beaming a smile at Liam.

"I should kick you out of my pub for what you're threatening to do to my family's property," Cait said, her eyes steely as she measured Dylan. "But, in this matter, I'll let Grace lead. Just remember: It's the lady's decision whether your butt is allowed to warm a seat in my pub. Understood?"

"Yes, ma'am," Dylan said, nodding his head and doing

his best to look like a choirboy. "I'm doing my best to stay on her good side."

"See that you do." Cait nodded once more before stepping briskly to the other side of the bar to fill more orders.

"She's mighty fearful, that one," Mr. Murphy mused, shaking his head after Cait.

"Don't let her hear you say that," Grace advised him.

He chuckled, tugging his newsboy cap lower on his head. "I may be old and half-blind, but dumb I am not," Mr. Murphy said.

"So, this must be Dylan."

Grace almost rolled her eyes at Aislinn who now stood, a small smile on her face, behind Dylan's stool. Dylan automatically turned and half-rose to offer her his seat, but she waved at him to sit.

"Sit, sit. I'm only here for just a bit."

"Dylan and Liam, this is my aunt Aislinn, a very famous and exceptionally talented artist." And reader of auras, empath, and overall badass, she added silently in her head, watching Aislinn size up the men while Grace popped the tops on a few bottles of beer and slid them onto a waiting tray. The pub was beginning to fill and one booth had been cordoned off for music. Though there was a small stage for a band, inevitably most people just shoe-horned their way into a booth and pulled out a fiddle and off they went. Grace lost track of Aislinn and Dylan's conversation as she was forced to work her way down the bar, smiling and laughing at the regulars who were delighted to see her on the other side of the bar for once.

In a matter of time, the tension eased from her shoulders and she began to enjoy herself. She could almost forget that Dylan was at the bar, he blended so easily into the fabric of the pub. She fielded yet another invitation to dinner from one of the lads watching the game, Ryan, who had asked her out once before. A sweet man, but not for her, Grace thought, letting him down gently and nudging him toward Mary instead, who actually had a liking for him.

"Pour yourself a wine, you're all done," Cait ordered. "Casey's arrived and taking over from here."

"Oh, I hadn't even noticed. Time flies when you're having fun behind the bar," Grace laughed, and bent to pull out a crisp white wine she'd been meaning to sample. "Looks like it's shaping up to be a fun night. Is that Shane in the booth there with the fiddle? I had no idea he played."

"Aye, he's been taking lessons – at his age! He's a real knack for it too. Who knew?" Cait beamed at her while her husband counted off a beat and the group of musicians in the booth launched into "Dirty Old Towne."

"I like him," Aislinn announced, coming to stand on the other side of the bar from Cait and Grace.

"Shane? I agree. Cait should keep him," Grace said, grinning cheekily at Aislinn.

"I've a mind to, and that's a fact," Cait said, beaming once more at Shane, who winked at her from where he played the little fiddle with ease.

"Ahh, interesting. She avoids the subject matter," Aislinn observed.

"Just because you're married to a head doctor doesn't mean you need to analyze me," Grace said, feeling grumpy at Aislinn's assessment.

"It doesn't take a head doctor to tell that you're both very interested in each other," Aislinn observed.

"She speaks the truth. Your eyes have been wandering to each other through the night. Both of you," Cait nodded, sipping from a glass of water.

"How can you like him when you know what he's trying to do to me? To Fiona's home?" Grace asked, arching a brow at Aislinn.

"His aura's pure. I think there are layers to all this. Talk to him," Aislinn advised.

"Nobody's aura is pure," Grace grumbled, ducking under the pass-through with her purse and wine.

"True. His isn't completely pure. But then he wouldn't be any fun, would he?" Aislinn twinkled at her and Grace rolled her eyes. "Go sit with them. They got a table so you could rest your feet once Casey came in. I'm slipping into the kitchen to snag some take-out, then heading home to snuggle that brainy man of mine."

"Send him my love," Grace said, kissing Aislinn's cheek and then scanning the pub to find where Dylan and Liam had sat. It didn't escape her notice that the locals all watched her as she crossed the room to sit at the small table they'd commandeered. Would she be sending the message that she now approved of this man? Her feelings and thoughts muddled, Grace plopped into the chair Dylan pulled out for her, nibbling at her lower lip.

"Tough shift?" Liam asked, his eyes on her expression.

"What's that? Oh, no, not at all. I always love helping Cait out. It's great fun," Grace said, sipping the wine and finding it to her taste. Sighing in relief at being off her feet, she stretched a bit, rolling one ankle around in the soft shortie boots she wore.

"It seemed like you had loads of fun. The male clientele certainly made a beeline for the bar," Dylan observed, his voice carrying an edge to it.

"As they should. I'm a favorite around here," Grace said smoothly, refusing to feel bad or apologize for flirting. It wasn't like the man had tried to make a claim on her. In fact, the only thing he'd really tried to do was woo her enough that he could succeed in his ultimate goal.

"Dylan used to tend bar back in the day. It's how he met his business mentor," Liam said, easily interpreting the look on his friend's face and changing the direction of the conversation.

"Is that so?" Grace asked, sipping her wine once more as the band took a break and the noise in the bar drew to a softer lull of muted conversations. "I suppose you'd find your mentor drinking his days away and teaching you such nefarious business practices as trying to strongarm the little guys to get your own way, no?"

She wasn't sure why she said it – a mixture of annoyance at Dylan for still not seeing her but still exhibiting jealousy over her actions, and just plain old frustration at the entire situation.

"If you're calling my business ethics into question, you've every right to contact all of my companies and customers. None of whom have anything bad to say about me," Dylan said, his voice icy. He leaned back and crossed his arms over his chest – arms that Grace so desperately wanted around her – and stared her down.

"Oh, I'm well aware. I've done my research on you,

Dylan Kelly," Grace said, still feeling the need to poke the bear. "You've led a careful life, no? Very philanthropic, a good head for business, and a long string of girlfriends with never a bad word to say about you. Which just makes me wonder... what's this man hiding? It's almost like you've led *too* polished an existence," Grace said, tilting her head to look up at him, casual as could be, though her words were like daggers.

Liam opened his mouth to speak, but thought better of it and leaned back in his chair to watch the show, as many of the other villagers were doing. Though Grace and Dylan didn't seem to notice, the pub had gone virtually silent in order not to miss what was turning out to be the evening's real entertainment.

"Being successful at what I do and being kind to my girlfriends certainly shouldn't lead someone to think I'm hiding something, in my opinion. If anything, I have nothing to hide – it's all on display, right? So you think you know me from what you've read in the society pages?" Dylan raked a hand through his unruly hair and downed half his Guinness in one gulp, slapping it back on the table with his first outward sign of anger.

"No, I don't think that, I *know*. Which is why I'm suspicious of who you really are and what your motives are in this town," Grace said, her temper simmering just below the surface of her words. "Someone who spends so much time carefully designing and curating his image for the public is clearly too scared to show his real self to people."

It was like waving a red flag at a bull, and it absolutely

delighted her to see fury cross Dylan's sinfully handsome face.

"Scared…" Dylan sputtered, his manhood grievously offended, at a loss for words for once in his life. "I have nothing to hide, doll."

"You're so used to getting your way that you're having a bit of tantrum now that you can't get what you want. I see the walls cracking. Where's the careful calm businessman now?" Grace all but shouted, having come to her feet. Dylan met her on the way up. They stood almost nose to nose, tension crackling between them like lightning in a heat storm about to break.

"This has nothing to do with me, and everything to do with you," Dylan said, his eyes narrowed in calculation.

"Of course it does!" Grace threw up a hand in frustration. "You think you can roll into town, sweet-talk everyone, and offer double the hourly wage just to get laborers to do your dirty work for you."

"I had to double my already generous wages because someone has been actively working to destroy my plans," Dylan pointed out, clearly miffed that he was having to pay more.

"As I should be! Don't think you'll be getting an apology from me. It's my life you're after ruining," Grace said, almost shaking as the full force of her rage slammed into her. Thunder rattled the building and the villagers all cast worried eyes to the ceiling. Grace was infamous for her temper, and most knew it was best not anger the woman if they wanted the weather to stay calm for the evening.

"And it's my dream you're trying to destroy," Dylan seethed, punctuating the words with his finger in the air.

"Some dream. Don't you have enough money lining your pockets?" Grace cried, beginning to hate herself for still being attracted to a man this vile.

"It has nothing to do with whether it's enough or not –" Dylan said, but Grace cut him off.

"Well, get used to parting with some of it, Dylan Kelly, because I'll have you know I'm suing you," Grace said, her face inches from his. Thunder rode on her words as shock sliced across his handsome features. Grace picked up her glass, drained the wine, and slung her purse over her shoulder. Without another word, she strode from the building, leaving an infuriated Dylan to stare after her, his mouth hanging open.

"Suing me? The nerve of that woman…" Dylan said, grabbing his coat from the back of the chair and racing after Grace. The villagers all cast a worried look at the door, back at Liam, and then as one turned to the natural leader of the pub, Cait.

She hauled a leather-bound book onto the bar, and brought out a zippered bag used for holding cash. Opening the book, she took a pencil in hand and looked up.

"My money is on them dating within two weeks," Cait said, pulling a ten from her pocket and dropping it into the bag. Liam threw back his head and laughed as people clamored to the bar to lay their bets on how long it would take for Dylan to woo Grace.

No wonder Dylan had fallen in love with this place, Liam decided, and pulled a twenty from his wallet. No reason not to get in on the fun.

CHAPTER 21

*G*race stomped through the rain to her truck, not caring that her blouse was getting wet. In fact, the fat drops of rain that plastered her hair to her shoulders and drenched her clothes seemed to cool skin that felt like it was on fire. Reaching her door, she wrenched it open, only to screech when it was slammed closed once again. Whirling, she held up her clenched fists.

"Suing me? You've already filed an injunction," Dylan shouted.

"Aye, and since I've caught wind of you trying to get the villagers to work for you regardless of the injunction, I realized that you'll stop at nothing to get what you want," Grace shouted right back.

"I have every right to build there."

"No, you don't. It's not your land. And if you can't feel that in your bones, you're an idiot," Grace declared, the rain coming down in sheets between them.

"You've a bad habit of insulting my intelligence," Dylan said, stepping dangerously close, forcing Grace's back to the truck.

"I call it like I see it," Grace said, her chin up.

"Yet you'll ignore this?" Dylan said, deliberately letting his gaze slide down her face to where her wet blouse, all but see-through now, molded to every inch of her curves. The rain did nothing for the heat that flashed through her now – this time from lust, not rage.

"Aye, I can acknowledge you're handsome enough," Grace said, "But I've no interest in a man who goes through women like they're some sort of delectable candy."

"Women are delicious, and I, for one, have no issue with tasting them," Dylan said, edging just a bit closer.

"Be that as it may, I've no interest in a man who flits from woman to woman like a distracted gnat," Grace said, putting her hand up to his chest to push him back. Instead, he grabbed it in his and held it there, the pulse of his heart beating beneath her palm.

"Liar," Dylan said, and Grace opened her mouth to protest, only to have it enveloped by his.

Oh, but she wanted to push him back. She hated when men thought they could take what they wanted from a woman. But... it was just a kiss. And she trusted him enough to back off if she really told him to keep his hands off. Plus, when it came down to it, Grace had enough power in the tip of her pinky finger to send him running.

And then she couldn't think at all.

Kissing him was like coming home. It was all of her

dreams come to life in one moment – the taste of him, his touch the same, but oh so different. In her dreams she had felt like she was back in those stolen moments in time with him, but the now was so different. So much more potent. Despite herself, Grace moaned as he changed the angle of the kiss, deepening it, pulling her down with him as the rain drummed over them.

Belatedly realizing where they were and just how many people could be peering out of the pub windows, Grace broke the kiss and stepped back.

They stared at each other and she wondered at the thoughts that stormed behind those magnetic blue eyes. Did he see her now? How could he kiss a woman like that and not feel what she felt? She searched his face for answers, but found none – at least, not the ones she wanted.

"Come home with me," Dylan said, his breath ragged.

"No," Grace said, shuttering her emotions and reaching up to pat his face lightly. He surprised her by turning a kiss into her palm.

"Why? Are you scared?" Dylan asked, mimicking her attack from earlier.

"Of so much…" Grace said, blessing the rain for hiding the tears that slipped into her eyes. "More than you can understand. Good night, Dylan. I'll ask you to stay off my land."

He let her leave, as she'd known he would. Despite the nasty things she'd said about him in the pub, the man had honor. It was she who, in this moment, wished she had a little less honor and could throw caution to the wind. Her body screamed for his hands on her, and she drove home with her mind clouded by lust and regret.

Even if she'd gone with him, although the night would have been fun, the morning would have been empty – and Grace prided herself on winning the battles she took on.

And wasn't true love worth a battle?

CHAPTER 22

*G*race had proceeded directly to her shower when she'd arrived home, allowing the steaming water to rinse away the tension of the night. By the time the water grew cold, Grace was spent. She crawled naked into bed, pulling a huge down comforter over her, and closed her eyes. With the sound of rain pattering on the roof and the warmth of Rosie cuddled at her side, Grace dropped right into sleep.

She'd gone to collect flowers that day. A silly endeavor, she supposed, for a pirate warrior. But Grace rarely had pretty things on her ship, as it was built for battle and for hauling goods. No sense decorating her captain's quarters with the finest things if they would just be broken. But – well, she had a great love for flowers. She considered them little balls of joy, popping up from the landscape, giving of their beauty freely to the world.

She'd been a bit more sentimental of late, Grace supposed, for having spent time with Dillon. Oh, but she loved the man! From the stories he told her over the fire each night, to the way he made her feel with his touch. There was nothing like waking up each morning cradled in his arms, seeing the sleepy smile spread across his face as he looked at her. She'd never known such joy in her life. Sure, she'd loved her first husband, and his death had saddened her. But – ever the realist – Grace had picked up and moved on with her life.

Bending, she snipped some clover and pressed it into the basket, humming as she went. She'd sprinkle the flowers around the cottage when she got back, tucking them in various corners and along the windowsill.

Today, Grace thought. Today was the day she would ask Dillon if he'd want to come home with her. Meet her children. See her home, her land – everything she'd built and battled for. She reckoned he'd like it, though she'd never try to make him stay. Grace recognized a wandering heart when she saw one, and she knew that the man would never be happy without the sea. Nor was she, if she was honest with herself. Maybe they'd take a few of those adventures together, she mused, and crested the hill. Following the path that led toward the beach where their little cottage was sheltered, Grace slammed to a stop.

The flowers forgotten, strewn behind her on the path, Grace ran, digging the dirk from where she always kept it in the waistband of the breeches she wore. Dillon had teased her for dressing like a man, but she knew he appreciated how it showcased her shapely legs. Breeches gave her a freedom of movement both on the ship and on land.

She screeched a warning to the two men who battled

on the beach with Dillon. Her heart thudded as he fell face-down into the sand and didn't move, didn't even try to get up.

"No..." Blind with rage, Grace didn't even give the first man a chance to speak before she drove the dirk directly into his throat, ripping it clean across and felling the man before she whirled, blood dripping from her hand, to face off with her lover's murderer.

"That's a pretty lass," the man crooned, his fine coat showing his station. Grace's eyes landed on the crest emblazoned on the pocket, noting the name of the clan. For if Dillon truly was lost to her, she'd never sleep until the clan felt her pain tenfold.

"Oh? Do you like what you see?" Grace said, dropping the hand with the dirk and shooting him a flirtatious look. When he paused, his sword hand faltering just long enough to smile at her, Grace dove forward, plunging the dirk into his heart and twisting it mercilessly. Not even watching as he fell, Grace turned and raced to Dillon, using all her strength to roll him.

"Dillon," Grace breathed, propping his head on her lap, tears leaking down her cheeks and onto his face. The blood... oh, so much blood. A stray gull cried overhead, its melancholy call so lonely, as Grace's heart shattered into a million pieces.

"Gráinne. My forever love. Now and always..." Dillon choked out, a sliver of blue flashing between almost-closed lids. "Across time. My heart for yours."

Grace pressed her lips to his, begging him to stay with her, proclaiming her love over and over.

But he was gone, lost to her forever. Ages later, when Grace finally stood, it was as a new woman – a hardened one – and she vowed to seek revenge on those who had stolen her light from her. Grace vowed that, from that moment forward, she would never let herself be so vulnerable again.

CHAPTER 23

The rough lap of a tongue across her cheek woke Grace and she turned, crying openly as Rosie desperately licked her face to dry her tears.

"Thanks, baby," Grace said, cuddling the dog close and taking a few shuddering breaths. Curling into her comforter, she took stock of what she'd just witnessed and felt in her dream.

So it had been true, then, what she'd read about Dillon being murdered. A part of her had hoped it wasn't, simply because she'd never dreamed about it. She'd been spared the more gruesome aspects of that time, and blessed with the joy. Now she wondered why she'd been shown his death.

Such a horrific death, at that. Grace shuddered again as she flashed back to the blood draining from his body onto her legs.

"Grace."

Grace turned to find Fiona at the edge of the bed, a worried look on her face.

"He was murdered."

"I'm sorry," Fiona said, her voice soft. "You avenged him, you know."

"I read something about that," Grace said, shrugging one shoulder. What did revenge matter when the love was gone?

"Aye, you went on to marry again, as women did in that time. It was more of a business agreement than a marriage, for it strengthened both of your political power. Even after you married, you went back and laid siege to the clan's castle. The clan who took Dillon from you."

A small smile flitted across Grace's face. It did sound like her. She couldn't imagine many men being happy with their new wife going off to battle to seek revenge for a murdered lover, but there was never a description that fit her better, she decided.

"Did I win?"

"Of course you did," Fiona scoffed.

"That's something, I suppose," Grace said.

"He kissed you," Fiona stated, perching on the side of the bed and peering into her face.

"He did. It was wonderful and maddening and… oh, I just wanted to scream at him to see me. All of me," Grace said, balling her hands into fists.

"Why do you think you were given this dream now?" Fiona asked, reaching up to smooth Grace's hair from her brow. Though Fiona was a spirit, Grace still felt the flutter of a touch across her forehead.

"Am I supposed to feel the pain of losing him? I already do. I never thought I'd find him and now here he is, right in front of me, and I can't have him," Grace said, her anger still simmering just below the surface. Fiona cocked an eyebrow as the patter of rain picked up outside.

"He's not lost to you. Not yet, at least," Fiona pointed out.

"Then maybe it's because I feel lost? Or that I'm at battle? Except in all reality, I feel stuck. Trapped. I want him… oh, I crave being near him like he's a drug that will heal all my problems. And then I remember that he's trying to take this land from me and tear down our cottage and I hate him. Why does he have to be this way? Why couldn't he have shown up in a different man? In a man who isn't trying to take the things that I love most from me?" Grace demanded, the injustice of it all making her want to scream.

"I think everybody shows up in your life for a reason. We all have different lessons to learn from each other," Fiona said, standing once more, happy to see the color back in Grace's cheeks. "Don't you think there's a lesson here for you?"

"Judging from how I felt in the dream last night, it's to protect my heart at all costs. I'd rather never love that hard again than open myself up to that much pain," Grace admitted.

"That's a damn shame, Grace O'Brien. I never took you for a coward." Fiona blinked out of sight before Grace could respond, so shocked was she at her great-grandmother's words.

Coward? That was the last thing she was. Obviously Fiona didn't have a clear view of the situation at hand. The reality was that Grace needed to protect her heart and fight for what was hers. The reality was that sometimes you just couldn't have it all. Better to play it safe, keep her walls up, and save Grace's Cove.

"And if I have to grow old alone and unsatisfied – so be it."

CHAPTER 24

"*T*he axle's broken," Liam said from where he stood by the digger. It had been sitting on a trailer since Grace had sent them hightailing off of her – scratch that, *his* property.

"Vandalism," Dylan said, shaking his head, though he wasn't surprised by it. As word of his project spread around the village, it seemed the opponents far outweighed the supporters.

"Maybe. 'Tis a tricky and difficult thing to break, though," Liam said, running his hand over his beard as he thought about it. "It's secured on the trailer quite well, and to even get on the trailer, crawl under, and – then what? What angle are you leveraging a tool large enough to snap an axle? And one of that size? I'm really struggling to understand how this happened."

"Parts must be rusted. You know how it is living close to saltwater," Dylan said, his tone terse as he moved down the sidewalk. The morning had dawned brisk, with a light chill in the air, but he was happy to see that the rain, which had plagued them for days now, had finally subsided.

He'd spent much of yesterday holed up in his house, reading books, researching the history behind Grace's Cove, and doing his best to push the infuriating Grace O'Brien from his mind. Unfortunately, he'd failed at the last part and had spent much of the day mooning around the house wishing she was there for him to battle with. Or to engage in other more lively diversions.

The village hummed around him with the Monday morning bustle of children being packed off to school, markets opening, and people heading off to work. The scent of a proper Irish fry-up wafted to him from a diner he passed, and Dylan's stomach grumbled in response. If his boat weren't set to dock soon he'd have stopped for a breakfast, some tea, and a chance to look over the paper. Instead, he was on his way to meet some of the workers he'd managed to bribe into working for him – and the men who were already loyal to him – at the docks for a quick meeting on what they hoped to accomplish this week, with the added benefit of being able to keep his eye out for *The Pirate Queen.*

The name still made his stomach clench every time he recalled Grace casually saying she was no mermaid, but instead a pirate queen. Though he'd resolved himself to believe that she was toying with him, a deeper side of his subconscious seemed to press at him as though it knew he was lying to himself. If he was being totally honest with himself – something he usually tried to do – he would admit that he didn't see Grace as being that crafty. For she'd been genuinely surprised when he showed up at her house with gifts, and he doubted she would have used that moment – especially before she'd even fully woken up – to try and mess with his head.

Still. It had to just be a coincidence. It wasn't that uncommon to talk of pirates, especially when one lived on the water. She'd likely just plucked an idea from the air and spoken without thinking. It meant nothing more than that.

"It's a brand new digger," Liam said, bringing him back to the conversation, though he had noted Dylan's distraction.

"Then it's vandalism. Just because we don't know how it was done doesn't mean it wasn't vandals. Remember, we've got a target on our backs here, right?"

"Aye, vandalism it is then," Liam said, affable in the morning sun that struggled to peek through the clouds. He even had the audacity to whistle a little tune as they walked past storefronts painted in cheerful colors.

"Is there something you'd like to say?" Dylan ground out, annoyed at his friend's response.

"You're the boss. If you're comfortable with claiming vandalism, that's fine by me, boyo," Liam said, a smile hovering on his lips. Dylan narrowed his eyes at him as they dodged a group of schoolboys, dressed in their uniforms, racing up the sidewalk chattering about the hurling match from the weekend before.

"Liam, I don't have the patience for this today. Just speak your mind," Dylan said. He'd had another night of fitful dreams, torn with lust, half in love, with Grace as the star of the show.

"I'm just thinking back to the other day when the

trucks starting honking and dancing all on their own. Just wondering if there's other hijinks in the air is all," Liam said, holding a finger up and swirling it in a little circle in the air.

"Is this about magick again?" Dylan pinched his nose and sighed.

"You're not one to ignore all possibilities, are you?" Liam asked, cagily dodging the question.

"I'm not, no. But... I think this whole 'enchanted curse' thing is going to everyone's heads. My guess is that there is a very logical and reasonable explanation for all these events," Dylan said as they drew close to a group of men – a smaller group than he'd hired – who huddled at the dock.

"If you say so, boss," Liam said, clapping a hand on Dylan's back before striding forward to greet the men.

"I swear I don't know why I'm friends with you," Dylan called after him, only to receive a shit-eating grin over Liam's shoulder.

Briefly, he turned to scan the harbor. The sea was calm today, with just a light breeze to ruffle his hair, and it was business as usual for the fishermen on the water. His boat should have been here by now, Dylan thought, especially on such a calm day. Wondering what the holdup was, but trusting his crew, he turned back to join the group that waited for him.

"Seems we have some more issues," Liam said, tucking his hands in the pockets of the fleece jacket he wore.

"Morning, gentlemen. What seems to be the problem?" Dylan asked, smiling at each in turn. A few shuffled their feet, some hunched their shoulders, and, aside from the crew he'd brought with him, most averted their eyes.

"Well?" Dylan asked again, when the silence drew out.

"Ryan's car won't start. John has the flu. Derek had an allergic reaction to something he ate and is covered in hives. David's tools are missing. Erik can't find the keys to his toolshed or for any of his construction equipment. Ron's power has gone out at home and the water isn't running in Sean's house," Liam recited quickly, and Dylan was reminded once again why he'd hired this man to be a project manager. He doubted he would have been able to remember each man's name so quickly, let alone all the particular worries that plagued each of them this morning.

"Well, now, that's quite a litany of problems, is it not? Tell me… is a certain red-haired woman who lives near the cove bribing you to be coming up with these issues?" Dylan asked bluntly. The shock on their faces was enough to have his answer.

"No, sir. We need the money, that's the truth of it. Look, I even came when I'm sick," Derek said, pulling his shirt up to reveal a thick rash of hives that covered his stomach.

"And you still came in for work? That's a good man," Dylan commented and pulled Liam a few feet away.

"I've heard of this happening before. It's like… I forget the name of it," Dylan said. "But when the whole village believes something, they all get sick or they all think it is a curse, and things happen because they all believe it." Dylan stopped, realizing that he was danger-ously close to babbling.

"If you say so, bossman," Liam said, still way too

cheerful for Dylan's liking.

"Just pay the men their day's wage and send them home. Let them know I'll contact them when the work is ready."

"No problem," Liam said, turning to speak with the men. They protested, for all of them preferred doing an honest day's work for their wage, but finally Liam was able to convince them to take the money for their trouble and wrangled a promise of their future cooperation when the work was ready.

"Don't even say it," Dylan said, when Liam finally joined him where he stood, scanning the horizon for *The Pirate Queen*.

"Wouldn't dream of it," Liam mused, pulling a thin cigar from his pocket and lighting it, content to let the silence draw out between them as they watched the boats bobbing far out in the harbor.

Dylan's thoughts whirled. Sure, his mother had always delighted in all things magickal and fae, but it seemed so far removed from reality. At least the reality he lived in.

"There's an explanation for this. I suspect the village is just banding together to try and run us out of town," Dylan finally spoke.

"And the hives?"

"Happenstance. An easy excuse," Dylan said, shrugging.

"And if it's not?" Liam asked.

"Then I know just the witchy-eyed woman to confront," Dylan grumbled.

"That's a lad," Liam said, and clapped him on the shoulder.

CHAPTER 25

"If you're certain, Grace, I'll draw up the papers today," Martin said, measuring her over his desk.

"Oh, I'm certain. Seeing as I shouted it in front of the entire pub the other night," Grace said, and Martin was kind enough to pretend to be surprised.

"Is that so?"

"Oh, don't act like you haven't heard. I swear gossip travels faster than the speed of light in this town," Grace said, plucking at a loose thread in her pants. She'd done nothing but field phone calls from various family members and friends all day long yesterday. The blessing had been finally getting a chance to speak with her parents, whom she'd assured several times that they didn't need to leave their cruise. After she'd promised for the gazillionth time that she would have them come home if the situation escalated, as well as the promise to send them copies of all litigation-based paperwork, she was able to get off the phone with them. Cait's daughter Fiona had taken a bit longer to persuade.

"Fi, you're living it up right now. Do not come home," Grace had insisted.

"Then you come to me," Fi demanded.

"I feel like leaving now would probably be a bad idea," Grace said gently, and laughed when Fi groaned on the other end of the line.

"Duh. You need to be there to kick his arse into line. And then to kiss his wounded male pride when you dominate him," Fi decided. Grace laughed once again, picturing her friend drinking Limoncello on the Amalfi coast and having what she sincerely hoped were many a flagrant affair.

"I promise I'll visit soon. Let me sort this out first."

"Keep me posted on this Dylan. I think he's the one for you, Grace. Don't discount all the history you have," Fi said, worry lacing her voice.

"I'm not discounting it. But I think I need to learn from it. It hurts too much, you see? I can't love or live with the possibility of losing like that again. I'm happy with my life now. I love where I live, I love helping people, and I'm over the moon with everything going on with my business line in New York. I've no reason to muck it up with a man. You know I'm more than capable of scratching that itch when needed," Grace said.

"Be that as it may, I think you'd regret not giving this a chance," Fi said, and Grace could all but feel her worry push through the phone.

"Bulldozers, Fi. Remember them?"

"Right, right. Bulldozers. Got it." Fi had signed off with the promise to call later in the week. Grace had spent the rest of the day ignoring her phone and working on the first stages of the battle she'd decided to enact against one Dylan Kelly.

"I'll admit that I heard wind of an altercation," Martin said, drawing her back to the conversation at hand.

"Martin, I don't think there's any way around this. He's determined to have his land, and I'm determined to keep what's mine." Grace held her hands up in despair.

"Then I'll be happy to draw up the papers for you. It will take a few days, and of course we'll have to formally serve him and his counsel," Martin said, then paused, his face lighting up.

"What?" Grace asked, looking around her.

"It just occurred to me – the man needs permits passed, no? For his building and whatnot?" Martin looked at her owlishly across his desk.

"And? I'm assuming he's secured the proper permits," Grace shrugged.

"Well, usually there's more than one permit that's needed. It's a process as a build-out happens. Inspectors go out and so on." Martin waved his hand in the air. "If there's a challenge to the permit or, say, any litigation that's brought before the Village Board... There's a council meeting, you know. Anyone can go. And lodge a protest."

"Well, now, would you look at you? I had no idea you had this side to you, Martin. I quite like it," Grace said, delighted with the man.

"It's all aboveboard, of course. I'm just calling it to your attention, if needed." Martin cleared his throat, but a faint blush of pleasure tinged his cheeks.

"And what happens if the whole town goes to the meeting?"

"Depending on how many complaints there are and the like, it can go past a Board vote to a village vote. Frankly, I don't think we've had a village meeting where we all voted in years," Martin mused, rolling his pen between his fingers as he leaned back and thought about it.

"Sounds like it's high time for another meeting, don't you think?" Grace smiled sweetly at him.

"Well, we do so like to chime in with our opinions on matters," Martin agreed, breaking into a smile.

"You're the best, Martin. A saint among men. I'll get the town gossips on this little tidbit right away," Grace said and breezed out the door, barely remembering to say her goodbyes to a pleased-looking Anne. Her first stop would be the pub, Grace decided, for it was just nearing lunchtime and she could at least get the ball rolling. It was only a short stroll from the solicitor's office, and Grace all but danced down the street.

At Rosie's sharp bark, Grace looked up to find a decidedly angry-looking man heading right in her direction, his long legs eating up the ground between them until he stood, a breath too close to her.

Refusing to step back, Grace raised her chin until she met Dylan's eyes.

"Can I help you?" Grace asked, amused at the frustration she saw in those gorgeous sea-blue eyes of his.

"That's kind of you to ask, Ms. O'Brien," Dylan said, deliberately addressing her by her surname. "There is something you can help me with."

"Go on," Grace said, hands on hips, chin raised.

"I don't know what little games you're playing, but you've no reason to get the town to vandalize our equipment," Dylan said, watching her closely.

"I didn't," Grace said, not missing a beat.

"You're telling me that you aren't responsible for our equipment breaking?" Dylan asked, his eyes narrowed.

"I'm telling you that I didn't, and wouldn't, encourage anyone in town to break your equipment," Grace said, neatly sidestepping his question.

"But you aren't saying that you're not responsible?" Dylan asked, too smart to let her get away with that.

Grace looked away then, and noticed they were once again drawing a crowd. A group of women, ready for lunch at the pub, waited on the sidewalk across the street and watched them, avid interest on their faces.

"I'm responsible," Grace said, knowing at heart she couldn't lie to him.

"How?" Dylan demanded.

"You wouldn't believe me if I told you," Grace said and took a step to move past him. When he grabbed her arm, she paused and looked down at his hand until he let it drop to his side.

"Don't try to tell me it's this enchanted cove curse nonsense. I get mysticism and magick and all that, but this is a bit much," Dylan said, frown lines appearing in his forehead.

"Okay," Grace said, with a small shrug, and began to walk. She was used to dealing with skeptics, and had found that instead of trying to explain or justify her beliefs or what she knew to be true, it was easier to simply let them believe what they wanted. It wasn't her job to prove herself – to anyone.

"Wait, that's it? Just 'okay'?" Dylan said, blocking her once more as she tried to pass. Grace rolled her eyes and blew out a sigh.

"Yes, that's it. Is there anything else?"

"Have dinner with me."

It wasn't what she'd expected him to say, and it certainly seemed it wasn't what *he* had expected to say, judging from the surprised look that crossed his face.

"No, thank you," Grace said, politely letting him off the hook.

"You owe me," Dylan demanded.

"I do not," Grace argued, annoyed to find them once more facing off in front of a growing crowd of people.

"You admitted you're responsible for my equipment breaking. For my part, I'm willing to let the cost and damages of that slide if you have dinner with me," Dylan said.

"How would you prove that I damaged your equipment?" Grace tilted her head at him.

"Your word."

Caught – Grace typically was an ethical person, though she wasn't against some nefarious tactics in battle – she sighed.

"Fine. Come to the cottage for dinner."

"Nope. I say when and where. I'll be in touch."

Frowning after him, Grace felt unsettled, like she couldn't get her sea legs under her. Which was what the man wanted, she reminded herself, and turned into the pub, ready to spread the word about the town meeting. She was still at war, after all.

CHAPTER 26

"*Y*ou want me to meet you at the harbor?" Grace asked, pulling the phone away to look at the screen in confusion. She hadn't given the man her number, but someone – and she could imagine a few sneaky someones – had given it to him.

"Yes, at five o'clock, please," Dylan said.

"That's a tad early for dinner, no?"

"You'll survive," Dylan said, and ended the call quickly. The man was obviously still annoyed with her for the havoc she'd wreaked on his equipment and his crew, but Grace didn't feel bad about it.

Granted, when it came to her magick, she usually stuck with the centuries-old practice of harming none. Causing the flu and hives to hit her fellow villagers was technically harming someone – however, she'd remedied it straight-away and had even added a boost of extra magick to speed them on their recoveries. She'd gone around herself to both of their homes and made certain they were right as rain. In turn, and as penance, she'd taken the illnesses into herself and had then suffered the consequences of both the flu and hives on her body. She'd spent the rest of the day in bed, and had a miserable night, but had woken with no sign of either illness except for the deep shadows under her eyes. Fiona hadn't bothered to stop by while she was sick, but Grace was actually thankful for that.

She didn't need someone pointing out her stupidity, thank you very much.

She wasn't perfect, Grace thought, as she spent the morning running some rituals over a new cream she was concocting to soothe colic. A friend of hers was struggling with a particularly colicky baby and Grace felt better for being able to do something positive for the world. Truth be told, she didn't feel good about enacting the magick she'd done yesterday. Even though she'd paid the price for it, it sat uncomfortably on her soul.

"I suppose I'll need to fight fair moving forward, Rosie," Grace said to the dog, who was chewing on her bone, happy as could be. Grace needed to learn to be more patient. If she'd only waited to enact her magickal pranks until after she'd met with Martin, she would have had a smarter and more ethical way to fight Dylan on his own level. Now she'd had to deal with a nasty bout of the flu, was operating on little sleep, and would have to eat crow and apologize to the man at dinner. A dinner that she wouldn't have been guilted into going to if she hadn't caused trouble to begin with.

Pleased with the way the cream turned out, Grace bottled it and put it aside to drop off at her friend's on the way to dinner. Glancing at the clock, she realized she'd have just enough time for a wee nap before getting ready for dinner. Grace wasn't at her best after a night of no sleep, and it probably wouldn't be smart for her to arrive at dinner even more on edge than she would normally be. Making up her mind, she invited Rosie into her room and quickly slid into sleep.

She was delighted to awake from a dreamless sleep, refreshed, and with just enough time to get ready for dinner. Grace wasn't sure she could have handled another dream of Dillon before dinner tonight.

Dress for the elements, the man had said.

She didn't want to overthink it, Grace decided, as this was most definitely not a date. It was best she go in with a business attitude, find out what he was up to, and then get out. She pulled on skinny jeans, a bright blue sweater that highlighted her eyes – she wasn't opposed to using *some* of her wiles – and a necklace that had been passed down from Fiona through Keelin, and now once again resided with her. Grace held the amethyst to the light, admiring the stone and remembering the ancient healer woman who had pressed it into her hands centuries ago. As stones went, it probably held very little monetary value. But the power it held and the love it was infused with were priceless.

"You're here for the night, my love. But I'm sure Fiona will stop by to visit with you," Grace said, tucking a few treats into the toy bone Dylan had brought and giving it to a delighted Rosie, who sauntered off to curl up with her prize. Winding a scarf around her neck and slinging her canvas coat over her arm, Grace looked down at herself.

"That's as good as it's going to get."

On the drive to town, Grace found herself unaccountably nervous, which wasn't a feeling she was used to, or frankly allowed herself to feel. She'd spent her whole life plunging headfirst into anything she wanted, without giving a second thought to any consequences. It was always act first, consequences later. But this? This felt important, like something she could very easily screw up. Failure was not something Grace would accept.

She almost breezed her truck right past him, so lost in thought was she. Ignoring the little jump in her stomach when she looked at him, Grace eased her truck to a stop and hopped out.

"Going sailing?" Grace asked lightly, with a nod to the harbor where they stood.

"That's exactly what we're doing," Dylan said, walking toward her, his handsome face serious. He looked wonderful, Grace thought, with a heather grey sweater, dark jeans that she was certain would make his bum look amazing, and his tousled blond hair. He hadn't shaved for a few days and his light beard completed the look of a man comfortable at sea. It took all her power not to sigh in longing.

"You don't just buy boats, then, you run them as well?" Grace asked, thanking him when he took her coat and wound his arm through hers. There were the nerves again, she thought, as they strolled like a companionable couple down the planked walk that led to the docks.

"I suspect you know that I sail. What with all your research on me," Dylan said. Ah, Grace thought, someone was still mad about that. For some reason it cheered her, knowing she'd gotten under his skin.

"One must research one's opponent. You're a business-man. You can't tell me you don't put considerable time and effort into researching your competition," Grace said, tilting her head up to look at him.

"I can't say that I don't," Dylan admitted and Grace drew to a stop, pulling her arm out from his and turning to look at him. She needed to get this out of the way – opponent or no – or she'd let the evening slide by without apologizing.

"I…" Grace began, and Dylan looked down at her, patiently waiting for her to speak. "I owe you an apology."

"For what, exactly? The things you said about my character?" Dylan asked, quirking an eyebrow at her.

"For being responsible for some of the… uh… issues you had with your crew. I promise that, moving forward, I'll meet you on equal ground when it comes to our negotiations," Grace said, lifting her chin.

"Is that what we're doing? Negotiating?" Dylan asked.

Grace nodded. "I'd say it's a battle, but 'twas the first word that popped into my mind."

"And that's the apology?" Dylan asked.

Grace nodded once more, refusing to budge. A woman could only give so much, after all.

"Fine. Apology accepted. Now I owe you one," Dylan said, and Grace almost laughed.

"Whatever for?"

"For kissing you," Dylan said, his expression grave as he looked down at her.

"Oh, well. 'Tis no matter. You aren't the first to have stolen a kiss from me." Grace shrugged it away, feeling awkward about the direction of conversation. Dylan's face turned mutinous at the mention of others who had kissed her, which Grace filed away for careful reflection later on.

"I shouldn't have kissed you. Not while we are in…
negotiations, at least," Dylan said, raking his hand through
his hair. "It's unethical. For that, I apologize."

Interesting, Grace thought, as they turned to continue
walking. The man had a code of ethics that he didn't like
to violate. Yet he'd still kissed her – which meant he broke
the rules sometimes. The contrast appealed to the pirate
queen in her, for there were times when breaking the rules
was the only answer at hand. Not in this case, of course, as
there was no reason for him to kiss her. But she'd been
known to bend a few rules in her life and would likely do
so again.

"Did you rent a boat or do you have one here?" Grace
said, deciding to move past any discussion of kissing. She
wasn't ready to examine her feelings on that any further.
For now, she was trying to keep her enemy close. With the
village meeting coming up at the end of the week, their
negotiations would be coming to a head, and soon enough
Dylan would be gone. She'd deal with the aftermath of her
emotions then.

"Don't you know already?" Dylan asked, stopping so
that he stood in front of her and blocked her view.

"How would I know?" Grace asked.

"My boat was delayed by some strange circumstances
along the way, and arrived later than planned. Luckily
everyone was safe," Dylan said, crossing his arms over his
broad chest as he stared her down.

"I honestly have no idea what you are talking about,"
Grace said, genuinely shocked. "I can't say that, had I
known you had a boat coming to harbor, I might not have
put a word in the harbormaster's ear about not letting you

get a slip here, but I promise you I would never mess with someone's ship or endanger the livelihood of a sailor. My father is a sailor. It's a code I live by," Grace said, holding her palm to her heart.

"That's right – Flynn is your father, isn't he? I've met him before," Dylan said, switching the subject neatly. "Why don't you use his last name?"

"Oh… um… my mother wanted to go matriarchal. She gave me O'Brien, and Dad had no issues with it. We are a fierce bunch of women in my bloodline," Grace said, wondering if he would make the leap from Grace O'Brien to Gráinne O'Malley.

"Since you were honest with me regarding your involvement with the mechanical issues my crew experienced, I'll take you at your word that you didn't try to cause harm to my vessel," Dylan said.

"I swear." Grace put her hand on his arm, finding the muscle there as hard as rock. "I may cause trouble sometimes, but I'll always take responsibility for it."

"Fair enough," Dylan said, and Grace could feel the anger slowly leaving his body. "There she is."

He turned and pointed, but Dylan wasn't looking at the boat. Instead his eyes were on Grace when she turned to look.

"*The Pirate Queen*," Grace whispered, the punch of it slamming into her. She brought her hand to her lips, trembling a bit as she realized there was so much she didn't yet understand about Dylan. If he'd named his boat that… was it possible? Did he remember their love?

"Aye, *The Pirate Queen*," Dylan said, still watching

her as he rocked back on his heels. "My first boat and the love of my life."

"Why..." Grace's mouth had gone dry and she swallowed past a lump in her throat. "Why did you pick that name?"

"I don't really know," Dylan admitted. "I'd say it came to me in a dream, but I suppose that's too fanciful."

"No." Grace turned to him and almost bowled him over with the strength of her smile. "I'd say that's just right."

CHAPTER 27

The Pirate Queen was lovely, Grace mused, as she handily walked around the deck. As comfortable on boats and the water as she was in her cottage, she played first mate and helped Dylan with guiding the boat from the slip. It was a lovely little sloop, a perfect first boat, and she handled like a dream. It was no wonder Dylan had purchased her for his first. And the name – Grace sighed as she gripped the railing and looked out over harbor. He remembered. Deep down, something in him remembered her. Now if only he'd unlock it, Grace thought.

"I thought we'd have a sunset sail and then anchor up for dinner," Dylan said as she moved back to stand near where he captained the ship. He'd angled the boat to catch a nice breeze and they cruised along at a light chop, the dusky light warming the scene.

"I'm fine with that," Grace said, perching on a low bench that lined the rail, closing her eyes for a moment to enjoy the gentle motion of the boat, allowing it to soothe

the jumble of emotions in her stomach. Confusion, lust, anxiety, anger... they all wrestled there like a pit of snakes.

"You must like being on the water. What with having Flynn for a father?" Dylan asked, and Grace opened her eyes to see him studying her. He looked so handsome at the wheel, the sleeves of his sweater pushed back to reveal muscled forearms, the wind tousling his hair.

"I love being on the water, in the water, near the water, hearing the waves at night... it all calls to me. It's soothing, you see? To my soul," Grace said, smiling a little at him. "My cousin, Fi, she's yearned for the buzz of the city – any city – and has set off to explore the world for a year, or who even knows how long. She loves the hustle and bustle, the new restaurants, seeking out the latest trends, finding new bands – all of it. But me? A week without the sea and I'd start to go crazy."

"I can identify with that," Dylan said, nodding at her. "I've always had a yen for being on the water. I love seeing new horizons, wondering what they'll hold for me. But I'm just as comfortable with staying in the same spot, so long as it is near the sea. The sea never grows old to me. She's just as interesting and moody as any city I've come across."

"She is, at that," Grace said, delighted with the imagery, "I love watching how the light plays across her surface, highlighting each new color. She's even more stunning in the middle of a squall. I'll admit to pulling on my slicker and standing cliffside in the middle of a tempest just to see her churn. I do love it when the sea has a temper."

"Perhaps not the smartest idea," Dylan said, smiling at her.

"I didn't say it was smart. But passion pulls me on a whim. I have a tendency to plunge forward with what I want to do and consider consequences later," Grace admitted.

"Not a very safe way to live."

"No, that it's not. But it's certainly exhilarating."

"We're going to lose the light soon. I'll get us anchored up," Dylan said, noting the light leaving the sky. "There's a picnic hamper in the hull. Would you mind retrieving it for me?"

Grace did mind, as she loved helping when a boat changed course, but her curiosity won out. Alone, she'd have a chance to snoop a bit.

The galley was kept tidy, as Grace would have expected. A quick peek into the rooms showed neatly made bunks, a tidy bathroom, and a storage area. Nothing overtly personal stood out to her and she wondered briefly if he rented this out to clients. Making her way back to the galley, she found the picnic hamper tucked on the narrow counter.

"Champagne is in the fridge if you'd like some," Dylan called down, and Grace turned, noting a bucket ready for ice. She found the glasses in the cupboard, then busied herself with pouring ice from the chest into the bucket around the bottle. She realized she'd need to make two trips up, and as she turned to go, her eyes landed on the wall directly behind where she stood.

A canvas – it looked to be an oil painting – hung over the small table and chairs. Grace didn't know how she had missed it, but tears immediately swam to her eyes, blurring her vision for a moment before she hastily swiped them away.

It was a beautifully rendered painting of their cottage. The little stone cottage they'd stolen away to and made love for hours in, where they had shared their passions, and where Dillon had lost his life. It had been painted in a time of storm; waves crashed the shoreline while a single bolt of radiant light shone like a benediction through the brooding clouds to light the cottage. Her fingers itched to touch the painting, to run her hands over every paint stroke, to feel what the painter had felt when painting this. Was the cottage still there? Had someone found it and painted it?

"Everything all right?" Dylan poked his head in from above.

"Yes, I'm sorry, I was just admiring this painting. It's really lovely," Grace said, forcing herself to tear her eyes away from the happiest place she'd ever known.

"Thank you. I don't paint much, but try to when the mood strikes," Dylan said, and held a hand down. "Hand me up that hamper, please."

Almost numb, Grace stepped to the counter and picked up the basket, handing it easily up to him while her thoughts raced. *He* had painted the cottage? How had he known? This wasn't the way things were supposed to go. Somehow she'd imagined that if she ever did meet Dillon again, it would be like one of those Nicholas Sparks novels where the characters rush to each other and kiss in the rain, promising their undying love for each other or whatever. Instead, she had the uneasy choice of trying to decide whether she should tell this man that he was her lover from another time.

You did kiss in the rain, her subconscious reminded her.

Grace's heart did a little flip once again when she climbed up top with the champagne bucket and found that Dylan had unrolled a checked blanket on the deck, and thrown a few cushions to sit on around it. He was busy laying out food and unpacking the hamper, so she had a moment to steady her emotions before he saw her.

"I hope you don't mind sitting on the deck. It's just easier all around," Dylan said with a smile.

"Nope, I don't mind. Less chance for things to go rolling off a table," Grace said, and Dylan nodded in agreement.

"I just put together a tapas-style meal, since I wasn't entirely sure what you ate. Just a bit of everything, really," Dylan said, hands on his hips as he studied his spread. A very generous spread at that, Grace thought, surveying the array of food before her. A variety of cheeses mounded one platter, several fruit options on another. There were nuts galore, several bread options, some thinly sliced meats, biscuits, scones, and even a few little jars of jelly and jams.

"I think you've got it covered," Grace laughed, and sat on a cushion, tucking her feet beneath her and setting the champagne bucket on the blanket. Dylan immediately took over the duties of opening the bottle with a loud pop and pouring her a glass of the delicately fizzing liquid. Finally comfortable with how everything was set up, he sat. Grace wondered if he was like that with his business projects as well – making sure everything was just so before he could finally relax.

"Sláinte," Dylan said, clinking his glass on hers before taking a long sip of his drink.

"This is nice," Grace said, always happy to give credit where credit was due.

"Thank you. I wasn't sure if you would show," Dylan admitted.

"I wasn't sure why you asked me. You seemed surprised at yourself," Grace said, picking up a small plate and adding a selection of cheeses.

"I was. As I mentioned before, I don't like to muddy the waters with business and personal."

"So is this business or personal?" Grace asked, holding her breath for a moment as she waited on his answer.

The angles of his face hardened in the light from the lanterns he had lit, and she watched conflicting emotions roll across his face. Oh, the man was stubborn, she decided. No wonder he didn't remember her – he probably refused to.

"I don't know," Dylan finally admitted, clearly unhappy with his answer.

"Fair enough," Grace said, sliding a sliver of cheese in her mouth. Deciding that she wanted to learn a little more about this man – at least the man in the here and now – she changed the subject. "Tell me, what drew you to the water? Why shipping and sailing?"

"As I said before, I've always been drawn to the water," Dylan said, crossing his arms over his legs as he leaned forward to sample some of the fruit. "But after learning just how difficult a life fishermen led, I decided there had to be another option for making a living on the water. It was happenstance, or perhaps just good luck, that I met my mentor when I did during university."

Grace cringed a little as she thought about the nasty things she'd said about his mentor, but Dylan had the decency not to comment on it.

"So he taught you the business of boats," Grace said, encouraging him to continue.

"That he did. He saw something in me, he said. He ran it all – fishing charters, tours, and the like. Met a woman later in life who whipped his business into shape. That's one thing he's always tried to tell me – that the right woman will only make my life and business better," Dylan smiled a bit, thinking about his mentor.

"Seems to me you've tried out quite a few," Grace said, and then bit her lip. She could never quite hold back her snarky comments.

"Just researching, so I know when I find the right one," Dylan said, so easily that Grace was torn between laughing or smacking him. In the end, she smiled.

"You're ridiculous," she grumbled.

"What about you? I can't imagine you don't have a trail of broken hearts behind you. Yet you're still alone. Why? Is it because you grew up here? What was that like?" Dylan asked, peppering her with questions and neatly changing the focus of the conversation from himself.

"I've done my best not to break any hearts," Grace said, silently adding, *because the loss of you broke mine so many centuries ago.* "Growing up here was perfect. How could it not be? I had free rein to roam the hills; I had family everywhere that I could stay with, play with, learn from. My mother and great-grandmother taught me in the ways of healing. I learned how to create beautiful and meaningful products that actually help people. My father taught me how to run and brand a business. I've been able to travel when I want, but no matter what, I always come back here. This village, these hills, this water – it's my heart."

"Tell me more about your business," Dylan said, shifting uncomfortably. She could read his unspoken thoughts from a mile away – now he was trying to take all this away from her.

"It's a line of all-natural health care products, and some beauty products as well," Grace said, deliberately skipping over the more hands-on healing she did around town. The man lived and breathed business, so she spoke to him about what he understood. "I'm set to launch in several stores in New York this summer. I've had a great response so far and am looking forward to growing the brand. I'll need to hire on as I grow, but for now, I'm managing it."

"That's wonderful. Congratulations," Dylan said, smiling at her.

"Thank you! It feels good, as I am sure you know, to build something of your own," Grace said. "You've built quite a bit yourself."

"I have, at that. I don't think I ever quite set out to build as much as I have, but I do like a challenge. Though I've slowed a bit, to be honest." Dylan shrugged.

"Getting old?" Grace teased, finishing her champagne and smiling her thanks when he filled her glass once more.

"Discontent, I suppose," Dylan said, shrugging a shoulder.

"It must be lonely on top," Grace observed.

"I'm fine, more or less. Good friends, love my family," Dylan said, his eyes meeting hers in the dim light.

"Sounds like a great life," Grace said, shifting a bit under his look.

"It is. I have nothing to complain about," Dylan admitted.

"And yet…"

"And yet, here I am," Dylan said, finishing his glass.

"Why did you come here, Dylan?" Grace said, allowing the frustration she felt bubbling inside her to rise to the surface. "Surely there are loads of other playgrounds for you to get your rocks off if you're bored. Why here?"

"To build a legacy," Dylan said, his face closing up once again.

"Why do you have to do it on my land?" Grace demanded, desperate for him to agree to leave her lands and home alone.

"Answer me this, Grace," Dylan said, his voice cool. "Are you mad at me for seeing an opportunity and seizing it, or are you actually mad at yourself for not taking care of your land and your property? For not checking to make sure the lease was renewed?"

Grace's mouth dropped open. Had this been another century, she would have had a knife to the throat of any man who challenged her so. Here, in this time and place, all she could do was sputter at him.

"How dare you? I'm the victim here. You big corporate

types always think you can prey upon the little people," Grace exclaimed.

"Hardly," Dylan laughed. "I followed all the rules and did my due diligence. There were no backhanded or shady dealings. It's on you to protect your land."

"Have no fear, Dylan Kelly, I plan to protect my land from you at all costs," Grace hissed, furious at herself for coming to this dinner with him – for allowing herself to like him even just a bit.

"Are you still planning to sue me?"

"Planning?" Grace scoffed, the light of battle in her eyes. "I am."

"Then screw it," Dylan said, and tossed his glass aside. In an instant, his lips were on hers, surprising her so completely that Grace froze for a moment before she drew in a breath to shriek at him.

And found herself pulled under by the sheer wave of lust and love that rolled through her.

Refusing to cower, Grace met him heat for heat, running her hands through his hair and arching her back as he broke the kiss and trailed his lips down her neck to nibble at the delicate skin at her throat. Heat raced over her skin, and Grace desperately wished she could pull her sweater off, bare her skin to the night sky and let him kiss every inch of her body. Before she could think further, his lips met hers once more, this time slowing the kiss, deepening it so that he nibbled gently against her lips and cradled her body into his.

Grace immediately felt protected – cherished even – as he kissed her as if she were the most precious thing in the world to him. His hands ran over her body, soothing her, but never taking any liberties. No, Grace thought, he might steal a kiss, but he wouldn't go past that without her permission. It endeared him to her, even when she wanted to hate him – when she wanted to pretend he was someone else. But beneath it all beat the heart of a man who loved her through all time. If only he would realize it.

Grace gently pulled away, bringing her hand to his cheek so he would meet her eyes.

"Why did you paint that picture?" Grace asked, surprising him.

"In the galley?"

"Aye," Grace said, staying where she was, cocooned in his arms, her heart hopeful.

"On a whim, I guess. The image had been stuck in my mind for months. I almost feel like I'd been there before, but I have no recollection of seeing it on any of my travels," Dylan said.

Grace nodded. Sadness washed through her and she lowered her eyes, breaking their gaze.

"Maybe you were there in another life," Grace said, ever so softly.

Dylan laughed and shook his head, nuzzling into her neck to kiss her once more.

"Doubtful. But maybe… who's to say. Maybe I did live there in some past life," Dylan said, distracting Grace as he nibbled at her ear.

"How did you feel when you painted it?" Grace asked, holding her breath and trying to ignore the feelings Dylan's kisses were stirring low in her gut.

"Like it was the best and the worst place ever," Dylan said, pausing and looking up at the sky as he tried to gather the words. "I know that sounds weird. But it's why there is a storm as well as sunshine. Happiness and pain, I suppose. A reminder of how quickly things can change."

As interpretations of a past life went, it was dead on, Grace mused. He'd captured the joy and love they'd felt there, and the pain and misery of death and loss. Even if Dylan refused to open his mind to see, his soul knew.

He wasn't ready, Grace realized, and gently disengaged herself from his arms. Slowly she stood and looked down at him.

"I'd like to go home now," Grace said, sadness lacing her voice.

"Grace... I –" Dylan began, his handsome face a mixture of lust and misery.

"Don't... Dylan, just don't. This is one huge mess. I shouldn't be out here with you. I don't know how we'll see our way around this. We're both stubborn, we want what we want, and neither of us will back down. The heat of the moment changes nothing about what's going on in our lives. It's smartest if you just take me home now," Grace said, rubbing her hands over her arms to console herself.

"I don't want to. I want to spend time with you," Dylan said, standing up so he could meet her eyes. "I think about you all the time."

"And I think about you too," Grace admitted, allowing him to pull her into a hug. "But unless you call off your project and sign the land back to me and my family, this can never be."

They didn't speak for the rest of the ride home. Dylan walked her to her truck and stood, holding the door, as she buckled herself in.

"I'd like to see you again. No matter what happens with our business situation," Dylan said, his face set in stubborn lines.

"See, you can separate the two – but I can't. My business *is* personal," Grace said softly. Then she turned the engine on and drove into the night.

CHAPTER 28

*G*race didn't see Dylan again in the days before the town meeting. Nor did she bother reaching out to him. At the very least, he was either kind enough or smart enough to stay off of her property and away from the cove. Grace figured they both needed a cooling off period. It was obvious they were drawn to each other, but only one of them really knew the reason why.

"Though the idiot would know if he'd just put his walls down," Grace grumbled. For the thousandth time she vacillated between not wanting to ever love that hard again, and wanting him to love her. It was maddening, and she figured even Rosie was getting sick of her moping around the cottage.

Martin had called just that morning to confirm whether she wanted him to move forward with the lawsuit. When Grace found herself experiencing some trepidation, she paused.

"You know what, Martin? Yes, I absolutely do," Grace had said, her resolve firm. It was time she remembered just who and what she was – a fierce woman who battled for what was right. There was no way around it; what Dylan was insisting on doing was wrong. It was time for Grace to channel her inner pirate queen.

"Then I'll file them. We'll have his counsel served tomorrow," Martin said. "I'm assuming I'll see you at the meeting?"

"That you will. It's going to be interesting," Grace said, her voice grim.

Steeling herself, Grace dressed with care, wanting to project power and confidence before the village. Selecting a cream-colored wool pencil skirt that went to just past her knees, a fitted deep red sweater with a delicate lace-edged collar, and nude pumps, she turned in front of the mirror. It looked just a little too… sexy, she thought and pulled her mass of hair back into a low bun, clipping it at the nape of her neck. Needing the extra energy, she slipped her amethyst necklace over her head, feeling it pulse against her skin as it poured its love and energy into her body.

"Rosie, come," Grace ordered and Rosie ran to her, the toy bone in her mouth, ever hopeful. "No, you're coming with me."

Grace fastened Rosie's fancy collar – a plaid one in shades of red and blue with a huge bow – and smiled when Rosie pranced around the room. There was something about her fancy collar that made Rosie know she looked extra special. Women were women, no matter the species, Grace thought, and checked the time.

"Come on, Rosie, it's time for battle."

CHAPTER 29

*D*ylan sat at the dining table of his rental house, brochures, folders, and plans spread out across the entire expanse. He'd spent the last ten minutes pacing, returning each time to look down at where his dream lay.

The last couple of days had been nothing but one headache after another for Dylan. Between feeling insurmountable guilt for kissing Grace once more while still needing to see through his passion project, he'd been driven to visit the whiskey cabinet more often than he'd like to admit.

She still didn't leave his mind.

Over and over, he replayed how her lips had felt against his own, her taste, the very essence of her seeming to fill him with light and love. It was like she'd flipped a switch inside him, and he'd gone from numbness to feeling all the emotions at once. More than once he wondered if she'd used some sort of magick on him. Reluctant to explore that avenue too much, Dylan had chalked it up to plain old infatuation. It was because he hadn't been with a woman for so long, he tried to tell himself.

His dreams had been increasingly chaotic, and he'd wake drenched in sweat, only remembering flashes of them. A beach. The cottage in his painting. Grace laughing as she rose over him and covered him with her body.

Dylan clenched his fists as he looked down at the papers spread before him. The Grace's Cove Cultural & Community Center. His people had done a good job with the branding, designing a neat little logo with a kid on a sailboat. All he'd wanted to do was build something that would give back to the community – and the land and water access at the cove had seemed like the perfect place at the time. Dylan raked his hand through his hair and closed his eyes, conjuring up the vision he'd been working on for months.

It was meant to be an all-inclusive community center. He wanted to offer everything from sailing to business classes, free to young and old alike. It would be a place where there were no barriers to entry and people could take the first steps in learning a trade or picking up a new hobby – it might even become a gathering place for retirees. It combined all of his loves at once – the sea, learning new things, and passing on the gift of mentorship to others. Now Dylan wasn't sure what he was willing to sacrifice to get something he had wanted so badly, but he was someone who was almost impossible to dislodge once he had dug in his heels. He was certain he was in the right – this was important, after all – but as the days went by it was becoming increasingly difficult for him to see what he was in the right about.

"They've done a brilliant job with it," Liam said, coming to stand by Dylan and looking down at the designs. He'd been watching his boss pace for the last fifteen minutes in silence and decided it was time to intervene.

"Aye," Dylan said, reaching for his coffee.

"I really don't think all is lost. Even if Grace is suing you. Let me ask you this – why does it have to be on the cove? Could we find a better spot for it?" Liam asked, knowing he could speak frankly with his friend. "Perhaps compromise a little? Make it a win-win for everyone."

"I don't know, Liam. I really don't. I don't know if it's because I'm stubborn and refusing to bend, but there's something that is making me stick to this, and on this parcel of land. I know I can be difficult or refuse to back down at times, but usually, at the very least, I can back up my reasoning for doing so. Would it be a million times easier for me to just switch the location and become the hero in town for making Grace happy while also doing something good for the community? Of course. So why am I not doing that?" Dylan said, turning to look at his oldest friend.

"Maybe you're worried that if you let a certain blue-eyed beauty get her way, you'll have no reason to spar with her?" Liam asked.

"But that would be a good thing, no? Then we could just get down to the business of figuring out our attraction to each other," Dylan bit out, sipping his now-cold coffee and rifling through a few more papers on the table.

"You're certain the attraction is mutual?" Liam asked and then held up his hands and laughed when Dylan leveled a look at him. "Hey, I understand that women find you irresistible. I'm just saying that maybe it grates a bit that she turns you down."

"Oh please, not all women find me attractive. However, I'm capable of reading when a woman is interested, and Grace definitely is responsive to me. To a point. Then it's like she pulls the door closed, locks it, and disappears from me. And I can't reach her," Dylan said.

"I can't say that I blame the lass. You've put her in a tricky position. She's drawn to you, but you're the one trying to take her land from her. From what I can tell with my deep understanding of human nature" – Liam smiled cheekily – "you've really left her no way out. You've boxed her in, but instead of capitulating as you expected, she's fought you back on every turn, and politely declined your personal advances. All in all, she's your perfect match."

"Wait... what? She's not... it's not..." Dylan said, rolling his eyes at Liam. The man always wanted to find romance everywhere he looked.

"I know what I'm seeing, don't I? I like her for you. Now, we must get going. It wouldn't do to be late walking into the village meeting where they're about to behead you. Oh, this is going to be fun," Liam decided.

Dylan just shook his head at him as he rolled the papers up and shoved them into a tube. "Why am I friends with you again?"

"Because I help you get your head out of your arse," Liam said, chuckling at Dylan's glare. "Did you ask Grace about her magick?"

"I did not," Dylan bit out, not wanting to think too much about it.

"What about the cove?" Liam said, not pressing the point.

"I didn't ask her about it either. But my research and speaking with other locals all brings up the same story – don't go there, enchanted or cursed waters," Dylan said, putting the papers in a knapsack and slinging a coat over his shoulders.

"I've uncovered a tidbit from the lovely artist at the gallery down the street. I bought two of her paintings – I was helpless to resist," Liam said as they left the house and made their way to the truck.

"Aislinn? Grace's aunt?"

"Yes, that's the one. An extraordinary artist," Liam said, climbing into the truck.

"What did you learn?"

"It seems there's a lot of lore linked to the supposed enchantment of the cove. In fact, I'm now dying to go visit with more of an open mind. They believe it to be Grace O'Malley's final resting place. Hence the name Grace's Cove," Liam said.

"Grace O'Malley?" Dylan asked, vaguely remembering some bits about her from his history classes.

"Yes, indeed. The infamous pirate queen."

CHAPTER 30

*I*t was a madhouse.

Grace had expected a good turnout, but she'd not expected what looked to be the entire village already seated and ready for the action at the town hall, which had been built just a few years back. With standing room only, people spilled out onto the street and voices rose to greet her and Rosie as they strode up the sidewalk.

"Cait saved you a spot up front," Casey said, giving her a quick hug and ushering her inside.

"I can't believe everyone is here already. The meeting doesn't start for a while yet," Grace said.

"It's the talk of the town. Nobody wanted to miss it," Casey said, acknowledging all the businesses that had closed for the day. There were probably poor tourists wandering the streets, wondering if there was some holiday that they didn't know about.

"Gracie!" Grace turned at the voice and almost dissolved in tears, so shocked was she to see her grandmother and grandfather hustling up the sidewalk, identical looks of concern on their faces.

"Nan, Papa!" Grace was enveloped in an awkward three-way hug by Margaret and Sean. They lived in Dublin and ran a cheerful boat tour and fishing charter business, and had recently taken a holiday – to Iceland, of all places. Grace hadn't expected to hear from them for at least another week or so.

"A little birdie told us there was some trouble down here, so we had the plane drop us at Shannon instead," Margaret explained, looking like a million dollars in a chic leopard-print coat, white blouse, and crisp black pants. Sean – as handsome as ever, with just a bit less hair these days – smiled down at her.

"You know we've got your back for anything, Gracie; you've only to ask," Sean said, patting her arm.

"I'm so sorry you came all this way. I think after the meeting today, everything will be fine. But we'll see," Grace said, so happy that they had come.

"Honestly, we didn't get many details. Something about someone trying to force you off your land. I never…! Some people think they can take all the liberties. They obviously have no idea that you've a real estate powerhouse in your corner," Margaret sniffed.

Grace bit back a smile. "Don't worry, Nan. I'm suing him," Grace said.

"That's a good girl," Margaret said, patting her arm.

"Well, I'll be!" Sean all but shouted, causing Grace to jump in surprise. She turned to see him striding away, the crowd parting for him easily.

"I swear, he just knows everyone. Everywhere we go,

he's chatting it up with someone," Margaret said, craning her head to try and see who her husband was currently embracing in one of those awkward man hugs with a double pat on the back.

"How does he…" Grace said, shaking her head in confusion until everything clicked into place.

"Margaret, Gracie…" Sean crowed, towing a surprised Dylan Kelly through the crowd. "This is Dylan. I've mentored him since he was just a young lad. He's gone on to do great things."

Grace heard roaring in her ears, and she thought for the briefest of moments she might just faint on the spot. How could he have not told her that her grandfather was his mentor?

"Oh, Dylan! I'm delighted to meet you. Sean has spoken of you so many times over the years. He's had nothing but good things to say about you," Margaret said, smiling when Dylan kissed her hand. Leaning in, she whispered in Grace's ear, "He's a handsome lad. And quite well-to-do. You could do worse for yourself, dear. I say we all have lunch after this."

"Nan…" Grace just shook her head, seeing the bomb coming from a mile away but not sure how to warn them.

"I doubt Grace will be wanting to have lunch with me," Dylan said, reading her perfectly, "seeing as she's currently suing me."

"What?" Margaret said, coming to attention and turning from one to the other. Sean stepped back, looking mortally wounded as he stared at Dylan with confusion and then disgust. Grace could only imagine how that must feel, to have his mentor look at him in such a manner after all these years.

"What have you done to my Gracie?" Sean said, stepping into Dylan's space and meeting him eye-to-eye.

"I swear to you I didn't know until this moment that she was your granddaughter," Dylan said. "And for that, I'm truly sorry. I never would have even leased this land had I known. I only ever came here because you spoke so highly of it. I thought I was just picking up a parcel of land in a beautiful spot. I couldn't have known what a can of worms I was opening."

Seemingly appeased, Sean stepped back, unsure now. He glanced at Grace.

"I've never known Dylan to lie, Gracie. Surely there's just been some sort of misunderstanding. Can't we all just work this out?" Sean asked, hope on his face that he wouldn't have to choose between the two – though family would always come first.

"We are. Inside. Meeting's about to be called," Grace said, sailing resolutely past them to where Cait waved to her from the front row. Grace was relieved to see that the whole first row on one side comprised her family – Cait and Shane, Aislinn and Baird, Patrick and Morgan, and others spread out, having chosen their side. There was a flurry of welcome when everyone saw Margaret and Sean, and the meeting was delayed a few more minutes while everyone said their hellos and settled in. Grace took the seat on the aisle, and Dylan took the seat directly across from her, Liam at his side with a stack of papers in hand.

In front of them, the council members – six of them – all sat at a long table, some blinking in confusion at the spectacle before them and others looking a bit excited about the drama. Grace didn't blame them. It was probably the most interesting council meeting they'd had in years.

"We are calling this meeting to order," Mr. O'Sullivan said, and the crowd immediately quieted down. "This is a special session of our town meeting and we are here to address the validity of certain building permits. The issue at hand is that while the permits have been passed, there is now a legal action being taken, challenging the legality of the leasing of the land. The question today is not for us to determine whether it was legal or not – that is left up to the solicitors to handle – it is whether the building permits should be revoked or put on hold until the complications surrounding this build-out are addressed. Does everyone understand that?"

The whole village nodded as one.

"To reiterate, it is not our place to decide if the leasing of the land was legal or not. We are here to decide if Mr. Kelly is given his building permits." Mr. O'Sullivan looked over his glasses once more. He'd once taught maths class and his stern looks could bring most of the village to silence in seconds. "Good. Ms. O'Brien, please proceed."

Grace stood and smoothed her skirt, turning to smile briefly at the crowd before addressing the council.

"It is my understanding that the law requires adequate notice when the long lease of land is expiring. Because no notice was given to myself or my family, the land shouldn't have been available to lease to another person. While I understand that Mr. Kelly thinks he's fairly leased the land, there is no record shown of notice been given in regards to the plot of land he's trying to build condos on."

A murmur of disapproval went up through the crowd at the mention of the word 'condos.'

"It is my belief that all building permits should be revoked so that Mr. Kelly doesn't do any sort of irreversible damage to the land or my property until the legalities of this situation are properly sorted. At that time, I suggest the town vote on whether they'd really like a swath of tourist condos marring our pristine coastline. Thank you for your time," Grace said, sitting back down quickly.

Her face burned with frustration and she refused to look at Dylan. It didn't have to come to this point, but the man refused to budge. She supposed it would have to be a lesson for him, that big corporate ideals aren't always best suited for small towns. The crowd behind her clapped and cheered, calling out a myriad of interesting insults to Dylan until Mr. O'Sullivan shut them down. Margaret patted her leg when Dylan rose to speak, his hands full of papers.

"May I approach the table?"

Mr. O'Sullivan nodded and Dylan approached, handing each of the council members some paperwork.

"First of all, I'd like to set the record straight on a few points which seem to have been miscommunicated," Dylan said, turning to address the crowd before zeroing in on Grace. It was hard to deny his charisma, Grace thought. He carried himself well and had an easy confidence as he spoke.

"It's not my fault if Ms. O'Brien wasn't notified by the government in regard to the lease being up. That's on the tax office. And we all know how they can be," Dylan said, and several people murmured their agreement.

Oh, he's good, Grace thought, very good indeed, getting the villagers to agree with him like that.

"Then I came along and saw a beautiful piece of property up for lease. I mean, you've all seen the property, no? Sure and you wouldn't begrudge a man for wanting to own a stretch of that coastline."

More murmurs of agreement, and Grace almost rolled her eyes.

"So I leased the property and notified the tenant that she would need to leave. Did I think too much about it? No, but I suppose I should have. I just thought this town would be excited about what I was trying to build here."

"We don't need condominiums," a voice shouted from the back.

"Ah, thank you, and I completely agree. I'm not entirely sure where that rumor got started." Dylan slid a glance at Grace, though it certainly hadn't been her who'd started the rumor. She'd just repeated it. "But the assumption that I plan to build condos is a huge misunderstanding. What I have plans to build and what my current building permits are for – as I believe the council already knows – is a community and cultural center. It will offer free classes such as business mentorship, sailing classes, hobby building, and so forth. We planned to create a place where retirees can go to volunteer their knowledge to teach the next generation, to pass on lessons, and to gather for games, learning, and to celebrate the great culture and history of this town. I fell in love with Grace's Cove the first time my ship pulled into harbor. I would never try to harm this place. I only wanted to enhance it."

With that, Dylan Kelly sat down to a stunned silence. No one was more shocked than Grace. She felt like she'd been played for a fool.

"If there is no further information to add, the council requests to adjourn for a week to investigate all paperwork and claims before we decide how to proceed," Mr. O'Sullivan said, perfectly reading his audience. He knew that if he made a decision – now that the crowd was split straight down the middle – there would be pandemonium. The village needed at least a solid week to discuss all the ins and outs of this cultural center – and frankly, just to dissect the new gossip.

"Meeting adjourned."

Grace stood and, refusing to look at Dylan, whistled for Rosie and stormed from the hall, refusing to speak with anyone. If Dylan thought he'd endear himself to Grace by withholding crucial information and then embarrassing her in front of the whole town, he had no idea who he was dealing with.

CHAPTER 31

*D*ylan fielded questions outside the hall until Sean approached him, shaking his head.

"Phew, boyo, you've gone and gotten yourself into some deep trouble with one of my most loved people in the world," Sean said as he and Dylan walked toward where they had always gone to discuss problems – the pub. By some mutual agreement, the townspeople gave them space, and Margaret strolled behind with Aislinn and Morgan. Cait had already gone ahead, reading the energy of the town correctly and knowing she'd have a big night to set up for.

"I didn't know she was yours. I truly didn't," Dylan said, miserable that he had caused pain to Sean's grand-daughter. It was just the icing on the cake of an absolute shite couple of weeks. Why couldn't he have just stepped back from this project altogether?

"I understand. Don't think I'd be sitting here having a wee chat with you instead of my Gracie if I thought other-wise," Sean said, commandeering two stools in the far corner of the bar, which was a clear sign for others to stay away. Cait sized up the situation and, making no comment, slid them two whiskies, neat.

"That's a fine lass," Sean said, raising his glass to her in acknowledgement. Cait, never one to be at a loss for words, hesitated in front of Dylan.

"Go on, say what you need to say," Dylan said, nodding his head at Cait.

"Grace is special. Don't let her shut you out – or run too far away. She'll build a wall up so impossible to break that it will be like she never even knew you. And that's the last I'll say of that," Cait said, snapping her mouth closed. "Sure and I see you sitting there, Donovan. I'm on me way, can't you see?" Cait cuffed the lad on the head, and he issued his apologies and waited his turn for a pint.

"Now, that has me wondering," Sean said, narrowing his eyes at Dylan. They bumped their glasses and took a sip of whiskey before Sean continued. "Is this more than a business matter? Are you and Grace involved?"

Dylan ran a hand over his face, feeling drained. He was so used to things just neatly falling into place for him that he had no idea how he'd ended up here, having made a complete mess of everything and pining after the one woman who currently hated his guts. He said as much to Sean and glared at him when the old man started laughing.

"Don't you give me that nasty look, young man. I've been waiting for the day when a woman would send you arse over end. I should've known it would be one of mine. Strong women, they are," Sean said, nodding approvingly.

"I'll admit that I'm attracted to Grace. She's a lovely woman. But my mind isn't really on romance. It hasn't been for quite a while now. I just wanted to come here and see this project through. I really felt like I could make a difference and build something lasting that would contribute to the community," Dylan said, sighing into his whiskey.

"There's always time for romance, son," Sean said.

"I don't like to blur those lines. It wouldn't be fair to her, you see? If I made a play for her, she'd think it was just to get her land. I've already overstepped my bounds." Dylan held up his hands at Sean's glare. "I promise, no more than a kiss. But for me, that's crossing boundaries, when it mixes business and personal. I would never try for more. You know how I feel about that."

"Aye, that I do. You've ethics, which is something I've always appreciated about you," Sean said, rocking back and forth on his chair as he mulled the problem over, "You know... Margaret left me for over twenty-five years. Took off to America, pregnant with Grace's mama. It took everything in my power to get that stubborn woman to love me again. But I've never regretted a minute of it."

"I didn't know that," Dylan said, sipping the whiskey and letting the burn of it numb his insides.

"Now, my Gracie's built of the same stuff – if not stronger. She'll go down fighting. I don't know what's all between you two, and maybe that's for the best of it. But I'll say this – pride goeth before a fall. A little compromise does a world of good. Go talk to her. Before it's too late."

"Twenty-five years, huh?"

"Twenty-five miserable years. I swear I've never met a more stubborn lot of women. Damn, I love them for it, too. Nothing in my life has made me prouder than being surrounded by and raising strong women who can stand for themselves. I'll tell you this – if Gracie decides you're it for her, that's an honor. She may be a difficult woman, but she's world class," Sean said, smiling at Cait when she slid them more whiskey.

"I've been nothing if not impressed with her," Dylan said carefully.

"And the… you know," Sean said, waving his finger in a circle in the air.

"The… what?" Dylan said, furrowing his brow in confusion and wondering if the whiskey had already gone to the old man's head.

"The extra stuff. Abilities and whatnot…" Sean trailed off and then clamped his mouth shut.

"I don't know what… are you saying…?" Dylan just couldn't bring himself to say the word 'magick' to his respected business mentor, and he sought around in his brain for another word.

"Never you mind," Sean said, clapping Dylan on the back and standing. "I see you still have much to learn. My advice? Talk to her. Now, my beautiful bride calls for me."

Sean disappeared across the room faster than Dylan could down a whiskey shot and he was left mulling over what the man said. Before too many people could begin to approach him, Dylan slid Cait some money and slipped out the door, no longer interested in charming the crowd.

There was only one person he wanted to win over to his side.

CHAPTER 32

*H*e found her by the water, staring down at the walls of the cove, the wind whipping her hair free from the loose bun she wore. Grace hadn't bothered to change. She was too keyed up from the meeting, and instead she stood at the cliff's edge in her skirt and blouse, watching as the water churned in anger far below her.

"Grace," Dylan said, far in advance so as not to startle her. Though he was certain she'd heard his truck door slam, he was uncomfortable with just how close to the edge of the cliff she now stood.

"You didn't have to come out here. Go celebrate with all your new friends," Grace said, shooting him an angry glance over her shoulder.

"Grace, I'm sorry. But I have a right to protect what I'm trying to build." Dylan realized it was the wrong approach as soon as she turned and stormed to him, as beautiful in anger as she was when she was laughing.

"And I have a right to protect what's mine. I'm

promising you here and now that you'll build on this land over my dead body," Grace hissed.

Dylan felt a shiver race through him at the thought of her death. "I'm certain we can figure out a solution," he began, and Grace glared daggers at him. He was certain she wanted to shove him, so angry was her expression.

"We could have, yes, if you had bothered to include me in your plans. Instead, I've been pushed aside and played for a fool," Grace shouted, and Dylan realized how wounded her pride was.

"I wasn't trying to make a fool out of you," Dylan began again, only to have Grace whirl around and cut him off.

"Then why didn't you tell me? You had so many opportunities to correct my assumptions. I asked you flat-out on your boat why you came here. Couldn't you have explained that 'building your legacy' didn't mean a condo building? You had a perfect moment to explain everything to me. But you chose not to. I don't understand," Grace said.

Dylan felt his stomach plummet at the shine of tears that slipped into her eyes. "Grace, honey," he said, stepping forward to try and gather her into his arms. He was shocked to find that an invisible wall had come up between them. It was like his hands were pressed to a wall of ice, and he dropped them immediately. Too concerned for her to even try to fully examine what that little burst of magick was, he tucked his hands in his pockets instead.

"Don't you 'honey' me. Don't you dare patronize me," Grace said, delivering each word like a pistol shot. "You liked having the upper hand and you played it beautifully to your advantage."

Now Dylan sighed and ran a hand over his face. Maybe he had, but not intentionally.

"Grace, I'm used to negotiations and dealing with massive shipping companies, corporations, and multi-level deals. It just comes naturally to me to wait some things out and reveal my cards only when necessary. It wasn't even intentional, my withholding the information. I just did what I always do, which was let people make the assumptions they want to make. You wanted me to be the bad guy, and I allowed it. But I didn't mean to hurt you and for that, truly, I'm sorry," Dylan said.

Being able to read his aura, Grace knew every word he spoke was true. But now she needed to examine herself – had she wanted him to be the bad guy? Why? Was it because she was furious at him for not recognizing her from their past life?

"I suppose it was easy for me to make you the bad guy," Grace finally admitted, though it cost her. "All I could see was that you were trying to evict me from my land."

"Which I see now is not going to happen. We'll figure something else out. It isn't worth the battle. Maybe the village will work with me on finding a new location," Dylan said, looking down at the cove. It looked suspiciously like it was shining an odd color of blue.

"Is the cove…" Dylan wasn't sure how to phrase it. Grace glanced down at the water and her lips puckered, almost as if she'd eaten something sour. Dylan saw the minute her walls went up.

"Pay no mind. Just some of that enchanted nonsense that you like to pretend is small-town craziness. I appreciate your being willing to work out a new location for your center, which I'm sure will be a smashing success and a much-needed benefit to the community. I wish you the best of luck," Grace said, every word precise and polite.

"And that's it?" Dylan asked, once more trying to step forward, and once more being hit by some icy block.

"And that's it, Dylan," Grace said, an impossible sadness filling her eyes as she searched his face, looking for something he wasn't sure he could give.

He watched her trudge across the grass – a stunningly beautiful woman dressed in red and white, Rosie at her side – and his heart plummeted. Despite himself, he felt like he was losing everything, even though he'd basically just been handed the permission he needed to build his center. Even when he'd compromised on the location, it still felt empty.

When Grace slammed the door to her cottage, the shining blue light from the waters of the cove far below him winked out, leaving him more confused than when he had arrived. Dylan no longer knew what it was he was fighting for.

CHAPTER 33

"I don't think this is a good idea," Dylan said, pausing in front of where Liam leaned against the truck, two stainless steel thermoses of coffee in his hands.

"Let's review," Liam said, motioning for him to hop in the passenger seat as he took the wheel. "First of all, you didn't sleep last night. You're infatuated with this woman, you refuse to see her for what she is – basically a badass magickal mermaid witchy healer woman – and she used magick on you in real time, as in real actual life, yet you still are trying to convince yourself that it was some natural phenomenon you can't explain. I mean, the cove glowed blue, for Christ's sake. How are you explaining that?"

"Bioluminescence," Dylan said, but even to him it sounded dumb.

"Right. And they just switch themselves off and on in the middle of the day to light the cove up? Not likely. You know as well as I do that they shine only at night," Liam said, driving handily along the cliff road that led to the cove.

"Fine, I can't explain it. But I can't explain a lot of things right now and it's messing with my head, if I'm to be completely honest," Dylan said.

"That's obvious. Let's start with the easy one. What's your issue with magick? You were raised Irish, so you've learned plenty of folklore in your time. Your mother delights in all things magickal. As a sailor, you're naturally superstitious and we both know there's been a time or two where we've seen something on the horizon that we can't explain. So what's the deal? Does it scare you?"

Dylan took a sip from his thermos before answering, contemplating just what it was about magick that seemed to shake him so.

"I'm not scared of it, necessarily. I don't like it because I can't explain it."

"You mean you can't control it," Liam pointed out.

"Aye, I suppose that plays a part in it. It's more comfortable for me to be the captain of my own ship," Dylan admitted, shifting uncomfortably in his seat. "And if there really is magick around me then I have no say in anything. It makes me feel like I have no will. That at any point magick can be used on me and it's not a level playing field."

"Sure and that makes sense," Liam said. "But don't most of these practitioners of magick and all that go by a credo of 'harm no one'? Isn't there a way to view it as an added bonus in your life? As in, it can help you, not hinder you?"

"Maybe, but frankly, I don't see that this matters all

that much. I don't see it playing much of a part in my life one way or the other," Dylan said, staring out at the water far below him crashing into rocks as gulls made lazy swoops in the morning breeze.

"If you want a life with Grace, it will," Liam said.

The thought of life with Grace filled Dylan with a warmth, something he'd never known before, almost like a puzzle piece clicking into place.

"I don't know how I feel about all that. I think about her constantly. A few weeks ago, I never even knew this woman. Now I see her in my sleep. She's driving me to complete distraction. Then there's part of me that thinks, if she really is magick, then how do I know she hasn't just put a spell on me? Made me fall for her?" Dylan said. He massaged his neck, where he was currently carrying all his tension.

"Ah, don't you see, my young friend?" Liam laughed, for though he was only two years older than Dylan, he liked to lord it over him as though he had all the wisdom in the world. "All women are magickal. That's what makes them so special. They don't need potions or chants or ancient rituals to weave a spell over you. It's done with a smile, or the way they smell like flowers, or the soft little noise they make when they curl into you in their sleep. They trust you with their hearts. And that, my friend, is a magick all its own."

"You've a poet in your soul," Dylan murmured, inexplicably touched by his friend's words. Liam had always been a romantic at heart, but had never settled for just one woman.

"I'm man enough to know that love, given freely, is the

greatest gift in the world. There's no reason not to celebrate it," Liam said, a light smile playing on his lips as
they pulled to a stop near the cove.

Despite himself, Dylan's gaze trailed up the green
expanse to where Grace's cottage sat, tucked against the
looming hills, looking for all the world like the perfect
spot to go home to. Although he owned several homes
around the world, he'd never seen anything as charming as
this little cottage. Whether it was the woman who resided
in it, or the cottage itself, it beckoned to him. If only he
could know that the door would open for him if he came
calling…

"Should we go tell her what we are doing?" Dylan
asked.

"And have her lose her shite on you once again? I
think not. I love women to pieces, but sometimes it's better
to ask forgiveness than permission."

Dylan knew that Liam was itching to go into the cove,
to see if he could really feel any of the energy there. The
man loved nothing more than an adventure, and finding
out if this cove really was enchanted rated high up on the
list of daredevil things to do. It was what made Liam a
consummate storyteller – not only did he have a wide-open
heart, but he was virtually fearless in everything he
took on.

"I want to just say this once more, even if it brands me
as a scaredy-cat," Dylan said, turning to look at his friend.
"But I don't think this is a good idea."

"We'll soon enough find out, won't we?" Liam said,
ever affable, as he climbed from the truck and hightailed it
to the trail that led into the cove. Dylan knew he was

moving quickly so that Grace wouldn't catch sight of him from her window, and stop them before Liam satisfied his taste for adventure.

Dylan approached the cove with trepidation. Visiting here on his own last time had not provided the best results, but hopefully with the two of them together there would be no incidents. He knew Liam craved some adventure, or to even witness some magick, but that was not the type of trouble Dylan cared to court.

The morning sun filtered through the entrance to the cove where the cliff walls almost met in a ragged C shape. The water this morning was calm, a brilliant blue – almost deceptively calm, if Dylan had to describe it. His pulse picked up as they approached the beach. In all respects, it was a picture-perfect morning with beautiful weather and an idyllic beach. So why had a faint sweat broken out on his brow?

"Liam, man, wait up," Dylan called, not realizing that Liam had picked up his pace and was virtually skipping in delight across the sand of the beach.

"Do you see this place, man? It's amazing! Heart-stopping! And not a soul for miles. Oh, I could spend hours here – no, days, camped out on the sand, cooking food over an open fire, making love to a good woman. Oh, yes, this is the place that dreams are made of," Liam called, spinning around.

He never saw it coming.

But Dylan did, watching it unfold second-by-second, in horrifying slow motion. He watched, helpless, as a rogue wave towered over his friend from behind, casting him in shadow, and then seeming to devour him. Dylan screamed as the wave appeared to toss Liam neatly up in the air, impossibly high, then his friend's body crashed down to the rocks below, broken and bent at an impossible angle.

He ran.

CHAPTER 34

*G*race had been in a particularly nasty funk all morning, so much so that even Rosie wasn't having anything to do with her mood and had taken herself off to lie on Grace's bed and stare out the window.

She knew she was sulking. No matter how many times she tried to tell herself that a strong woman would forget about Dylan and move forward with her life – she had all these amazing things planned for herself, after all – she just kept circling back to the emptiness she felt in the pit of her stomach at the loss of him. Which, she reminded herself, was exactly what she'd been hoping to avoid, because she didn't want to let a man hurt her the way Dillon had when he'd left her life forever. Hadn't she promised herself to keep her walls up? And yet here she was, moping about after the damn man once again.

Sighing, Grace pulled a sweater over her head and shoved her feet into her boots. Perhaps a walk through the garden to harvest some herbs would help with her mood.

Digging her hands into the dirt and inhaling the damp scent of earth never failed to center her.

At Rosie's sharp bark, Grace's head popped up. Rosie rarely barked with such a shrill note. Then the dog lost it, racing to the door, her small body vibrating in hysterics as she threw her head back and howled. Grace's eyes widened. There was trouble.

"Show me, girl," Grace commanded, opening the door. Rosie burst out like a race horse from the gate and beelined straight for the cove. It was only when Grace's eyes landed on Dylan's truck that ice raced through her blood.

Grace hit the top of the trail at a dead run, her eyes searching the beach as she half scrambled, half ran toward the bottom. When she saw Liam – his body broken and bent, Dylan kneeling at his side – her stomach plummeted. Liam had been nothing but kind to her, Grace thought, shooting an angry look at the waters – waters she herself had enchanted – as she skidded to a halt where Dylan knelt by his friend's side. All the color had drained from his face and his eyes, wide with shock, met Grace's.

"I can't... I can't move him. I think it's his spine. Help me." Dylan's voice cracked. "I don't know what to do. My cell phone won't work down here, I can't reach the paramedics. Please, help him. He's... he's a brother to me."

Rosie whined by her side, licking Dylan's palm and leaning into his legs.

"Please, may I touch him?" Grace asked, gently putting her hands over Dylan's and pulling them away from Liam.

"Don't... don't hurt him," Dylan said, his breath ragged as he struggled to hold back his tears.

"I won't, I promise. But I need you to give me some space so I can see what we're dealing with," Grace said, nudging Dylan with her hip until he sat back on his knees and watched her. Grateful that the fall had knocked Liam out, Grace closed her eyes and went deep within, not caring what Dylan would see or know. It didn't matter anymore, not at this point, if she showed all aspects of herself to him. He'd already shown her that he didn't trust her enough to be a partner to her – to share his truth with her.

Holding her hands out, she ran them over Liam's body, keeping them just above his skin, never touching him, but only feeling. It was as she suspected, and her mind reeled at the sheer amount of strength and knowledge it would take to heal this man. And she couldn't do it here. Turning her head to look over her shoulder at Dylan, she met his ravaged eyes.

"I can help him. But you have to trust me. Is this man your brother? Would you do anything to save him?"

"Aye, he's my family, my brother, my best friend. Whatever you need," Dylan pleaded.

"Then you have to promise me that you won't interfere with anything you're about to see. I don't… I don't heal using traditional methods. It may be scary, but we've no time to get him care. His light…" Grace clenched her hand to her chest. "It's dying, you see?"

"Save him. Please, Grace. I promise to not interfere."

"We have to get him back to the cottage. I have what I need there," Grace said and stood.

"But… can we move him? How? He'll be paralyzed, no?" Dylan stood, wobbly on his feet.

"You said you'd trust me. No more talking. I mean it, Dylan. One word and you can ruin everything," Grace said. Perhaps it was slightly dramatic, but she would need every ounce of her focus to heal the broken man at her feet. Closing her eyes, she began to chant, calling on the elements, the angels, and the goddess herself to lift this man and carry him home.

Dylan's shocked gasp didn't deter her. Instead, she grabbed Dylan's hand and continued to chant, never breaking her ritual, never losing her focus as they ran across the beach, Liam's broken body floating in front of them, her sheer will and the power of all her angels bringing him to her cottage doorstep.

True to his word, Dylan had remained silent, but when they approached the cottage he raced forward and opened the door. With magick alone, Grace carried Liam to Fiona's old bed and laid him gently onto the coverlet.

"Get the amethyst necklace on my bedside table," Grace ordered, and ran to the main room to gather all the elements she would need for what would be the hardest healing session she'd ever undertaken in her life. "Fiona, I beg of you, if you're near, I need you now more than I ever have."

Handing her the necklace, Dylan whirled around to see whom she was talking to, but Grace just shook her head and moved past him.

"Stay back. Don't touch me, don't touch him, and don't get in the way of my view out the window." If Grace didn't send the darkness somewhere physical, it would consume and kill her. As it was, she'd already be taking on something that would bring her to the brink of her own life.

"Is it worth it?" Fiona asked, coming to stand by Grace as she stood over Liam, her hands running gently over his body.

"It's my cove. My enchantment. My responsibility," Grace bit out, shooting a look at Fiona.

"Aye, it is. But he knew the dangers. Free will," Fiona said.

"Either help me save him or get out," Grace said.

Fiona nodded. Her Grace knew the consequences of what she was doing, and the decision was made.

"I'll help," Fiona said, and laid her hands on Grace's shoulders, pouring power into her like a pitcher full of minty lemonade – a golden zesty energy of refreshment – and Grace closed her eyes to channel the flow of it.

In moments, she'd gone completely under, almost trancelike, and focused all her power and magick into saving the broken man who lay before her.

CHAPTER 35

Though it felt like days, it was likely only a matter of minutes, perhaps an hour, that Dylan sat, frozen in place, his arms around a shivering Rosie, as he watched Grace.

He'd never seen such magnificence, nor frankly could he even understand what he was seeing. A golden halo of light seemed to pulse around her, quickly enveloping Liam, and the two of them seemed to shine in this almost otherworldly glow. Sweat poured from her brow, and he wanted to go to her and wipe her brow, or put a cold cloth on her neck, but he held himself back. Dylan had promised to not interfere, no matter what happened.

She was enthralling, at one with the universe and all its energies, and he had never been more in awe of anyone or anything in his life.

And yet, as the minutes ticked by, nerves started to rack Dylan's gut. What if she couldn't save Liam? Shouldn't he call the paramedics from the house phone? It would make sense to have them on their way, just in case.

Worried that he was failing his friend, Dylan shifted from where he crouched, deciding he would just sneak into the living room and place a call to the medics.

Liam's eyes opened.

"Oh, there he is," Dylan whispered, careful not to disturb Grace's flow, or whatever she was doing. The light began to build around them both, pulsing in liquid waves of gold, becoming so bright that Dylan threw up his arm to shield his eyes and Rosie whined and buried her face in her paws. For a brief second, Dylan's heart seemed to stop as the thought crossed his mind that maybe he was witnessing Liam's soul leaving his body.

When a dark cloud, almost like a swarm of bees, flew from Liam and out the window, a resounding crash shook the entire cottage. Dylan jumped up, Rosie in his arms, and looked out the window, unsure of what to do.

"He'll be okay," Grace said and Dylan looked to where she knelt now, her head to the mattress. Gingerly, Dylan crept closer to look down at Liam.

"Hey, mate. Sorry the scare. Guess you were right about the cove," Liam said, his face pale, but the same smile hovering on his lips.

"How... how do you feel? Are you okay?" Dylan whispered, bending to place Rosie on the floor, casting worried glances between Liam and Grace. He wasn't sure if he was allowed to touch, or interfere, but she said nothing, only stayed with her head bowed to the mattress.

Liam stretched and Dylan almost passed out with joy to see his body moving seamlessly – no paralysis, and no broken bones to be seen.

"I feel like I was hit by a truck, and I could sleep for a

week. But I'm okay. See to your woman," Liam said, nodding to Grace. "She needs you more than I."

With those words, Grace slumped to the floor, motionless. Dylan scooped her up on the fly and, after depositing her neatly on the bed in her room, he called the only person he could think of.

CHAPTER 36

$\mathcal{I}$t wasn't long before voices filled the small cottage. Margaret and Sean had unerringly found Dylan, who was hovering over Grace where she lay on the bed.

"What's happened?" Sean demanded.

"Liam was hurt. Gravely. She healed him," Dylan said, feeling slightly embarrassed by the explanation but too tired to care what they thought.

"Did she take it into her? Or send it out?" Morgan demanded from the door where she, Cait, and Aislinn were crowded.

"Um, out? Something dark went out the window and there was a huge crash," Dylan said, and the women seemed to collectively sigh in relief.

"Here, now, let us in, will you?" Margaret said, nudging Dylan back a bit. "We'll see to her. Check on Liam, please."

Reluctant to go, Dylan just stood there. He'd never felt so helpless in his life, or so completely out of his element.

"I don't want to leave her. She saved Liam. For me, she saved him. It's my fault she lies here like this," Dylan said, his eyes on Grace, who lay motionless on the bed but for the light rhythm of her breathing.

"She has her own mind, doesn't she? You didn't cause this, but I hope next time you'll be more careful in your choices," Margaret said, then shooed him back so that the women could crowd around the bed. Dylan watched as they all linked arms and laid their hands on Grace.

"Come, boyo. Let's check on Liam. Come, come," Sean said, pushing Dylan out of the room and closing the door behind them.

"But…"

"They're of the same blood. There's none stronger that can help her now," Sean said. They both entered the other bedroom to find Liam propped on the pillows, looking faintly dazed, but the color had returned to his cheeks.

"There's a lad," Sean said, smiling at Liam. "Haven't seen you for ages now. I wish I could say it was under better circumstances, but nonetheless, here we are."

"Sean, always nice to see you. Sorry for causing a scare," Liam said, his voice drowsy, but his eyes bright and alert.

"You're not living if you don't have a bit of a fright now and again," Sean said. Then, casting a look over his shoulder to see if any of the women were about, he leaned in to whisper, "Think a whiskey will shape you up?"

"Just what the doctor ordered," Liam agreed, and Sean disappeared into the other room.

"Liam…" Dylan said, his hand closing around his

friend's palm, squeezing it tightly. "You scared the shite out of me."

"Aye, I know. It scared me too, truth be told. I couldn't feel my legs. I thought I was done for, I really did," Liam admitted. "It hurt like nothing else I've ever felt before – at least the parts that I *could* feel. I think I just eventually passed out from the pain. What... what happened? It seemed like one moment I was on the beach and the next I was a crumbled mess on the rocks."

"You were. It was a rogue wave – an enchanted wave – there's no other way around it. Just tossed you in the air like you were a dog toy. It has to be quite possibly the scariest thing I've ever seen in my life," Dylan admitted, squeezing Liam's hand harder, "I thought you were gone. I... I may not say it much, but you're family, Liam. I don't know what I would have done without you. You're my best friend, my right hand man, my brother."

"To family," Sean interjected before the moment became too weepy, and handed out small glasses of whiskey.

"Sláinte," Dylan said, taking his down in one swallow. Though it burned a path straight to his gut, he still felt shaky after what he'd witnessed that day.

"How's Grace?" Liam asked, his voice strained.

"She'll be fine. Just needs to regain her strength. A healing like that will knock a body out for a time, is all," Sean said.

"Still don't believe in magick?" Liam asked, cocking an eyebrow at Dylan.

"I... I have no explanation for what I saw other than

magick, power of the universe, divine intervention. So no, I can't say that I don't believe," Dylan said.

"Smart lad. You can't be around these women and not believe in magick. It makes the world a hell of a lot more interesting, and that's a fact," Sean said, cheerful as ever.

Dylan just shook his head at the man's easy acceptance of the phenomenal events they'd just witnessed.

"I know you aren't in here serving that man whiskey after he almost died." Margaret's sharp voice had both Sean and Dylan ducking their heads.

"Aww, Margaret, the lad asked for it," Sean said, neatly throwing Liam to the wolves.

Figuring she couldn't harass him much after the ordeal he'd had, Liam smiled at her weakly. "That I did, pretty lady. Just a wee spot of medicine to get me sorted out."

"Well, since you're all sorted, get to your feet then. You're coming back to the village with us," Margaret ordered.

"Wait, do you think he should stand?" Dylan asked.

"I'm fine, I'm fine." Liam rose easily, proving his words.

"Nonetheless, we'll be keeping an eye on you in town. Dylan, you'll stay here with Grace," Margaret ordered, and sailed from the room with her head high.

"But… wait. What if she needs something? Like something magickal that I can't do? Should I take her to the doctor?" Dylan protested, coming to stand in front of the women in the living room.

"We've done what we could to help her. All she needs now is rest, and to know that she's not alone. There's some soup from the freezer defrosting on the stove," Cait said briskly. "Make sure she rests."

"But…" Dylan said again, but his protests went unheard as the women steamrolled him before clucking around Liam and getting him to the car. In a matter of moments, the cottage was once again quiet but for Rosie, who came over and dropped the bone he had given her at his feet.

"I suppose that's the least I can do for you," Dylan said, remembering it was the dog who had found them first. Finding the cookie jar on the shelf, he tucked some treats into the toy before poking his head in to see Grace, resting peacefully in her bed beneath the eaves. It took all his willpower not to go to her, crawl in bed, and cradle her to his chest. It wasn't her job to soothe his nerves right now, Dylan scolded himself. Easing the door closed just slightly, he turned back to the room. Spotting the rocking chair and the fireplace, Dylan set about making himself at home.

For if he had any say in it, he wouldn't be leaving here any time soon.

CHAPTER 37

*S*he felt powerless.

It wasn't a feeling that Grace particularly enjoyed, especially considering she'd been able to do anything she wanted her whole life. At this moment, she was so exhausted that even opening her eyelids was a struggle.

Someone was moving around in her cottage, with soft music – a pretty Celtic number – playing from the stereo by her fireplace.

"Water?" Grace whispered, her eyes still refusing to open. Paws hit the side of the bed, and Grace felt Rosie's cold nose on her arm before she padded away. Seconds later, Grace felt a presence over her.

"Water?" Grace whispered again, hopeful.

"There she is," Dylan said, and he crooned to her as he lifted her head, pressing a cup to her lips so she could drink. The cool water soothed her ravaged throat and she smiled, just barely, before drifting off once more.

The next time she woke, Grace was able to open her

eyes. Turning, she saw that Dylan had pulled the rocking chair close to her bed. He sat there reading a book, Rosie at his feet. Dark circles ringed his eyes, and he looked like a man who was dead on his feet.

"Is there... water?" Grace whispered again, and Dylan's head shot up. Snapping the book closed, he sat on the bed and helped her with water once more. This time, she didn't drift off immediately, and instead surveyed his face.

"Thank you," Grace said.

Dylan half-laughed, raking his hand through his mussed hair and shaking his head. "You owe me no thanks. 'Tis I who should be thanking you. You saved Liam's life. I'm forever indebted to you," Dylan said, his voice sober as he looked down on her.

"I'm glad to have been of help. My responsibility," Grace said, still barely able to speak, her eyes drifting closed once more as her body demanded sleep to restore her resources.

The third time she woke, Grace was startled to find that Dylan lay in bed next to her, his arm thrown over her body, cocooning her in his warmth. Feeling incredibly safe, she snuggled in, and he buried his face in her neck. Grace held her breath for a moment, wondering if he would say anything, but then realized he was asleep as well. The man must have been exhausted, Grace thought, and settled back to enjoy the feel of his arms around her. Even if it was but for this one moment, she'd take it, and worry about what the future held later. Once more, she drifted off to sleep, feeling secure as she snuggled into Dylan's warmth.

Grace didn't know how much time passed before she finally sat up and looked around. She smiled at the sight of Dylan sitting in the rocking chair once more, his head nodding as he slept over the book in his hand. Not wanting to wake him, she slid her legs from beneath the quilt, for she desperately needed to use the facilities. Rosie, the little traitor, let out a short bark and Dylan snapped awake.

"What are you doing?" he asked, jumping to his feet. He was at her side immediately.

"I, um, need to use the toilet," Grace said, nodding to the little bathroom in the corner.

"Oh, right," Dylan said, and helped her up. Together they walked across the room, though Grace didn't need the assistance. She just liked touching him.

"I'm fine to go in alone. Truly, I feel much better," Grace said and smiled at him.

"You're certain?"

"I am. I haven't slept that peacefully in years. In fact, I'm quite energized," Grace admitted.

"You'll call me if you need me? I'll be right here," Dylan said, worry crossing his face.

"Yes, I promise," Grace said and slipped inside. One look in the mirror made her change her plans, and she laughed when he complained from outside the door.

"You didn't say you would shower," Dylan yelled.

"I need it. It makes me feel better. I promise I'm okay," Grace said as she luxuriated in the feel of the hot water coursing down her back. There was nothing quite like a hot cleansing shower after feeling sick for days. When she walked out, wrapped in only a towel, Dylan stood in front of her with his hands on his hips.

"You could've collapsed in the shower and hit your head," he griped.

"I really do feel better. In fact, is there any food? I'm ravenous," Grace admitted.

Dylan sprang to action. "Yes, let me make something. Can I help you to bed or… um, to get clothes on?"

Grace bit back a smile at his awkwardness, so uncharacteristic for this highly confident man.

"Why don't you get food and I'll put some clothes on."

"Pajamas only. You're going right back to bed," Dylan ordered as he left the bedroom. Which was fine with Grace – she wasn't quite up for leaving the cottage just yet.

Slipping on loose flannel pants and a long-sleeved waffle knit shirt, she toweled most of the dampness from her hair before winding it into a knot on her head. By the time she'd finished, she was more than ready to crawl back under the covers of her bed. Rosie jumped up immediately and pressed her nose to hers.

"I'm just fine, girl. I promise. It was scary for a moment, is all. You should get a badge – a hero-dog badge," Grace said, rubbing Rosie down until the dog rolled in delight on the bed.

"So, Rosie was the heroine of the story?"

Dylan came through the door with a tray. Leaning over her, he put the tray on her lap and she was delighted to see toasted cheese sandwiches and a bowl of tomato soup. Perfect fare for someone on the mend, she thought, and immediately dunked her sandwich into the soup and took a gleeful bite.

"Yes, I've never seen her like that," Grace said, gesturing with her sandwich, Rosie's eyes following its every move. "She completely lost her shite, howling away, and I knew instantly something was wrong. I opened the door and she was off like a rocket to the cove. When I saw your truck... I thought it was you."

Grace shivered as she relived the moment, and Dylan came to stand over her, running his hand down her arm to soothe her.

"I'm a complete and utter fool," Dylan admitted and Grace nodded, not trusting herself to speak without crying. She shoved another bite of sandwich into her mouth before she said something stupid, like 'love me.' Dylan hovered over her, awkwardly watching her eat, unsure what else to say. By the time she was finished, he'd made her so nervous with his fluttering about that she wanted to snap at him.

"All done?"

"Yes, mother," Grace said, feeling cranky.

A ghost of a smile passed across Dylan's exhausted face. "I'm told that once the patient gets cranky, they're on the mend," he said, removing the tray and then standing over her once more. "What can I do for you? What do you need?"

"A hug," Grace whispered, not willing to meet his eyes.

"I can accommodate that," Dylan said and the bed dipped as he slipped beneath the quilt beside her, pulling her to him so that he completely enveloped her in his arms. Burrowing her face into his chest, Grace listened to his heart beat. She wanted this – just this – more than anything else in the world.

"I'm so sorry. I should have stayed away from the

cove. Liam wanted to go there so desperately – I told him it was a bad idea. I knew it was a bad idea," Dylan said, his voice all rumbly in his chest.

"Men never listen," Grace said.

"I could say the same for many a woman I know," Dylan said.

"I suppose that's true as well," Grace admitted, shifting so she could look up at him.

"You scared me," Dylan said, his voice soft.

"My healing or the aftermath?" Grace asked, wanting to clarify.

"All of it. From the cove chewing Liam up and spitting him out, to you somehow transporting him home, to the healing, to you folding in a heap at the floor when it was done. It was the single most terrifying and awesome experience in my life. I'm still reeling from it all," Dylan admitted.

"Magick scares you," Grace said. It wasn't a question.

"It does. It makes me feel like I don't have a choice in the outcome of a situation," Dylan said.

"You always have a choice. Free will," Grace whispered, her eyes drifting closed as she snuggled in, sleepy and sated from her meal. She knew they had much to discuss and that nothing was really, truly resolved.

But in this moment? She was exactly where she wanted to be.

CHAPTER 38

*G*race blinked her eyes open, startled to see it was dark. Dylan lay next to her, his arms still wrapped around her, protecting her even in his sleep. She studied him in the low light from the small lamp on a table across the room.

She loved him.

There was no denying the fact. She could hide from it, disavow it, try to convince herself that she couldn't love the man he was in this lifetime. But no matter what tricks she tried to play on herself, the truth was always there, riding just below the surface. Grace loved him and could forgive him his transgressions of the past few weeks, if she so chose. He certainly hadn't handled things well, but learning how he had wanted to create something to help others had only endeared him to her further.

He'd stayed with her. Grace smiled, remembering how cute he'd looked bringing her soup and how terrified he'd been when she'd gone to the bathroom. She couldn't say what the future held, for her powers thankfully didn't lend themselves to fortune-telling. But Grace knew that whatever happened, she wanted him in this moment.

Reaching up, Grace trailed a hand over Dylan's cheek, and when his eyelids fluttered open, she smiled.

"Hey," Grace whispered.

"Are you okay? What can I do for you?" Dylan asked, instantly in protective mode.

"Kiss me," Grace whispered.

Delighted when he didn't hesitate, Grace slid into a kiss so gentle, so endearing that she never wanted it to end. When he drew back, she knew he would end it there – and that was the last thing she wanted. For in this moment – in their own little cocoon, the world at bay – she would claim her love for him.

Rolling over him, she pulled her shirt off and straddled his waist, her hair tumbling down from its knot and raining over her shoulders.

"Grace…? You're still recovering. You're too delicate right now," Dylan said, though she could see and feel just how she was affecting his body. Lust filled his eyes as his gaze dropped to her breasts and then trailed back up to her face.

"I'm full of life. I've been in bed for days. I have nothing but energy," Grace laughed down at him.

"You're certain?" Dylan asked, once more striving for control.

"Aye, I'm certain," Grace said, then squealed when Dylan's control snapped. In seconds he'd flipped her and begun kissing his way over her skin, his lips leaving a trail of heat as he found every sensitive bit of her body – from the nape of her neck, to the side of her breast, to a particularly sensitive bit on the back of her thigh. Squirming under his assault, Grace felt languid heat pool low in her belly. Delighted with him, she pulled his shirt over his head and ran her hands over the muscles she'd ached to get her hands on for weeks.

"You're magnificent," Dylan breathed against her thigh, his lips tickling her skin. She arched her back as he worked his way up, finding her most sensitive of spots, and gently, ever so gently, teased her beyond reason. Grace shuddered beneath him, begging for release, and his hands dug into her thighs as he finally and mercilessly sent her over the edge. Crying out, Grace barely had a moment before he'd worked his way up her body once more, finding her lips with his own.

"I want you… more than anyone I've ever wanted," Dylan said softly against her lips, teasing her as he brushed his hard length against her, once, twice, before sliding deeply into her. For a brief moment, Grace was saddened that he wasn't ready to use the word 'love' – but she hadn't used it either, she reminded herself. And then she could think no more as Dylan fit her body with his own like they were made for each other. Together they rode the storm, their gazes locked as they broke at the same time, a thousand words left unsaid between them.

After, Grace cuddled into him, his arm automatically curling around her, her head on his chest.

"Grace, how can this be? It feels so right being with you. Yet I've only known you but a short time," Dylan said. "Do you… do you feel the same way?"

Grace turned so that she lay on his chest, her head pillowed in her hands, and met his eyes.

"Aye, I feel the same way. Dylan, don't you remember me?" Grace asked, her eyes hopeful on his.

"Remember you? Have we met before?" Embarrassment crossed his handsome features, a sheen of sweat from their lovemaking glistening on his forehead.

"Yes," Grace said, ever so softly. "In another life."

"In... in another life." Dylan shrugged. "Sure, then I guess maybe we did meet. But I suppose you could say that of anyone."

His words hurt, more than he could have realized. But instead of throwing a fit like she normally would have, Grace took a deep breath.

"Not just like anyone else. Not us. We loved each other, very deeply, in another time. I've waited for you," Grace said, her eyes never leaving his.

"You've waited for me? Grace, how did you even know it was me? Or about a past life? I don't understand," Dylan said, and she saw his walls going up.

"You gave me a gift, in the cove, of your trust," Grace said, reaching up to link her fingers with his. "Will you trust me once more? To show you something?"

"Yes, I suppose," Dylan said, and she knew he was uncomfortable.

"You see, I started dreaming of you, once I'd grown into a woman. It was the same dream, over and over, for years. It was of us – us in another time, but our souls together. Every night, I'd dream of the most wonderful time with you – these stolen moments – and every night you'd promise me we had a love that transcended all time," Grace said. She wasn't able to bring herself to tell him that he had been murdered and taken from her. "Do you know where the dreams were set?"

Dylan just shook his head, his eyes wary.

"The picture of the cottage you painted. That was our home, for but a moment in time, and we loved each other fiercely there," Grace said, smiling at him, hopeful he'd see the connection.

"But how?" Dylan asked, his brain still searching for a logical answer. "I think I just painted that from …" He stopped.

"From a dream you had," Grace finished for him.

"I don't know if I can believe this. I'm still trying to wrap my head around everything over the past few days," Dylan said. "Please know I'm not dismissing you. It's just… a lot to process."

"I can show you," Grace whispered.

"You can time travel too?" Dylan exclaimed.

Grace chuckled against his chest, amused with him. "No, I can dreamwalk with you. Would you come with me? In our dreams?" Grace asked. "And I'll show you."

Dylan thought for a moment, and then nodded, pressing a kiss to her head.

"If it's a dreamwalk the lass wants, it's a dreamwalk she gets."

CHAPTER 39

*T*his time, when she walked up to him on the beach where he fished, it was as if they were in the now.

"Grace."

"Dylan," Grace said, smiling up at him and then sweeping her arms around to encompass the beach, the little stone cottage, and the wonderful privacy they had.

"You're so beautiful," Dylan said, wading from the water and smiling down at her. "I like those breeches on you."

"Thank you, my handsome man," Grace said and laughed when he swept her into his arms, carrying her into the cottage where he proceeded to love her the way her soul ached for. Afterward, curled in his arms, she looked up at him.

"I don't understand my feelings," Dylan said, surprising her. Reaching up, Grace smoothed his hair back from his forehead and searched his achingly blue eyes.

"How so?"

"If this is supposed to be the happiest moment in my life, with a love that transcends all time, why do I feel..." Dylan sighed, frustrated, and narrowed his eyes as he searched for the word. "...sad? A part of me, being here in this moment with you, feels incredibly sad. Why is that? It just doesn't make sense to me." He absently pressed a kiss to her forehead, pulling her closer as his mind sought the answers that he knew she had.

"Because you've asked – and because I've told you that you can trust me – I'll show you. But, Dylan, please remember our love. Here in this moment. Because what I show you next will be traumatic. I've had to relive it, and I hate that you will now, too," Grace said, her eyes filling with tears. But he needed to know the full story if he was to understand the depth of her love for him.

"It's going to be bad, isn't it?" Dylan whispered.

"Yes," Grace said, a sob catching in her throat.

"Then let me hold you, just like this, for a moment longer. Just a moment. And then I'll be ready to face what may come," Dylan said. Grace breathed his scent in, praying they would make it through what would happen next – on the other side, in their world now – and closed her eyes.

It was as bad as she had expected it would be, even more so reliving it a second time – this time with Dylan in the now – and seeing him fall. The blood – oh, the blood seemed to seep into her soul as she sobbed once more for their loss.

When she woke, Dylan was gone.

CHAPTER 40

*G*race refused to wallow. Even though she'd had to relive the murder of her love in her dream once more, it had reminded her just how strong she was. Getting out of bed, she padded into the kitchen to put tea on.

"Grace."

Grace yelped, holding a hand to her heart, and turned to where Dylan sat. He had returned the rocking chair to the spot in front of the fireplace.

"I… I thought you'd gone," Grace said, a hopeful smile blooming on her face. Until she took in the fact that he was fully dressed, shoes on, car keys in hand.

"I am going," Dylan said. Shame flitted briefly across his face before he looked away from her face, obviously not interested in seeing the pain etched there.

"Love 'em and leave 'em type of guy, are ya?" Grace said lightly, crossing her arms over her chest. Dylan rose and came to stand before her.

"No, and if it seems that way I apologize. I certainly

never would have slept with you if I had known all... everything you've showed me," Dylan said, his voice stiff.

"I'm not sure I'm following. You're saying that, had you known we were lovers in a past life, you wouldn't have loved me in this one?" Grace said, fire flashing in her eyes.

"It just feels... I don't like how this makes me feel," Dylan said, running a palm over his face and beginning to pace. "It's like I have no choice. That this was all predestined for me or something. It makes me feel powerless. As if all my life choices haven't really been my own and somehow I've been led here, like some sort of puppet, to fulfill some kind of magickal destiny that I don't even have a say in."

"You're saying you think I just magicked your arse here to fulfill what I think is our destiny?" Grace said, carefully enunciating the words as rage filled her. The nerve of this man.

"I just feel like this was all decided for me. Where's my say? Nothing has gone my way since I've met you. I feel completely out of control, in over my head, and now I've learned this. How do you think it made me feel? Having to relive my own death like that? Having to lose you and the love I felt for you?" Dylan all but shouted, his face traumatized.

"How do you think it made me feel, watching you die like that? Over and over?" Grace parried.

"I don't know, Grace. You haven't told me. How does it make you feel?"

"Horrible! I love you and I'm left with having to repeat

that in my head as I sleep each night," Grace said, tears spiking.

"No, Grace, that's where the confusion seems to lie. You loved that man, centuries ago. You don't love this man. You're just transposing your expectations of another time on me," Dylan spit out.

"That's a lie. I've tried not to love you. I pushed you away, did I not? I told you to leave me alone. You kept showing up. I didn't manufacture any of this. I didn't want to love like that again, don't you see? I don't know if I can bear being that vulnerable once again," Grace sobbed, furious that he couldn't see what was right in front of him.

What he was walking away from.

"I don't like being vulnerable either. And I certainly don't like feeling like I've been a pawn in some magickal game," Dylan said.

"You're not a pawn. You've had free will all along. I didn't have a say in when or how I would see you in this life," Grace said, tears slipping down her cheeks. Rosie came over and sat her bum on Grace's feet, whining a little at her tears.

"It feels like I have no say in anything. I don't like this, Grace. I don't want to feel all this, or think that my choice has been taken away," Dylan said, "That I can't leave or choose my own path."

Unbearably tired, her heart broken into pieces once more, Grace pointed to the door.

"There's the door," Grace said, ever so softly.

When he left, without another word, Grace slipped to the floor and wrapped her arms around Rosie, crying until she couldn't cry anymore.

Eventually she wiped her cheeks and stood, and she vowed she would never let anyone make her feel this way again. For in the end, it had been her who'd been the pawn all along. Even knowing how much it would hurt to love Dylan and lose him again in this lifetime, she still hadn't built her walls high enough.

A lesson she wouldn't have to learn again.

CHAPTER 41

*D*ylan found his mother kneeling in the garden, humming a little as her cat batted at one of the flowers she was planting.

"Now, we've discussed this. You may look, but don't touch. These are not your play toys. If I see you digging these up, I'm not feeding you anymore. You'll be left to fend for yourself."

The fat orange tabby rolled on its back and looked up at Catherine, a picture of chubby innocence. Dylan didn't think it would hurt the cat all that much to miss a meal here or there.

"Mum," Dylan said, and had Catherine bouncing back on her heels, her hand at her heart.

"Dylan! Oh my, I wasn't expecting you. Are you home already? Oh, honey, I've missed you," Catherine said, bounding to him. A small woman with dancing blue eyes, she always greeted him with enthusiasm, much as she greeted anything in life. In some respects she had always reminded him a bit of a fairy – bouncing here to there with verve and enthusiasm.

"Is Dad home too?"

"He's gone for a golf weekend with the boys. I don't blame him, with this weather. It's been a few weeks since we've seen the sun." Catherine chattered away, pulling him by his hand into the house. His parents lived in a lovely two-story farm house, something Dylan's father still liked to grumble about, but which had completely charmed Catherine when she'd first seen it. Now, she had turned it into a showcase, with stunning gardens, a little hobby farm, and even an area for lawn games. Seeing as how she neatly beat his father at bocce ball every time they played, Dylan figured Catherine was coming out on top.

"Let me get the kettle on," Catherine called over her shoulder. He wound his way through a hodgepodge of furniture, intermixed with pots of flowers that somehow all made sense together, and into the bright kitchen with a beautiful marble center island. Just because it was an eighteenth-century farmhouse didn't mean she couldn't have modern tastes, Catherine had reasoned, and had immediately reno-vated the kitchen to make it a modern and welcoming spot for the home. Many a serious conversation had been held at the counter, and Dylan pulled out a stool, dropping into it and propping his face on his hands as he watched his mother putter around the kitchen, delighted he was home.

When she turned with a plate of biscuits and really looked at his face, she paused.

"Oh honey, tell me what's wrong. Is it the mermaid?"

"How'd you know?" Dylan asked.

"I just had a feeling. Tell me everything," Catherine said, putting the tea on to steep and pulling up a stool next to him.

So he did. By the time he had finished, Catherine had gone through her tea and was opening a bottle of wine.

"I think a nice glass in the garden while the sun goes down, no?" Catherine asked, and Dylan smiled at her. When he was with his mom, it seemed there was no problem that couldn't be solved over wine and a visit to her flowers.

Dylan carried their glasses to one of his favorite nooks of the garden, where vines twisted here and there. He headed for the lovely little mosaic table with its two chairs, and the fat cat followed them, presumably hoping they carried more biscuits with them.

"Sláinte," Catherine said, and they clinked glasses. Dylan smiled at her and waited to hear what she had to say.

"I have to say I'm a bit ashamed to know that I've raised a complete idiot for a son," Catherine began, pinning him with a look. Dylan choked on his wine as he looked at her in shock.

"I'm getting a little tired of being referred to as an idiot," Dylan said, his voice steely, "In other parts of this country people seem to regard me quite highly for my intelligence and business acumen."

"Oh sure, you've plenty of smarts there." Catherine waved all his accomplishments away with a little flicking motion of her hand. "But when it comes to affairs of the heart? You're not very bright."

"I don't think you're being very fair, Mum," Dylan

said, biting out his words. "Can't you understand what a shock this has all been to me? It's changed my life – my perception of the world as I know it – and left me feeling like I have no understanding of anything."

"I think that's a very apt description of love," Catherine said, nodding approvingly at him. "Perhaps you're not so dumb after all."

"I'm not... I wasn't talking about love." Dylan rose, frustrated, and began to pace in front of her. "I was talking about magick and destiny, and all this other stuff."

"And you don't think love is magick?" Catherine parried.

"Well, no, not really. I mean, it can feel magickal, I suppose, but it's not, like, real-life magick," Dylan said.

"Then you don't really understand love. It can move mountains, my dear."

"Yeah, yeah," Dylan said, upset with it all.

"Oh, my darling, precise, and logical son. I so wished this for you," Catherine laughed.

"You wished for me to be miserable?" Dylan asked, turning to glare at her.

"I wished for you to have magick in your life. Love and laughter, frustration and fights, and the essence of being truly alive. The fact that Grace has real magick is only icing on the cake, as far as I'm concerned. How lucky are you to have found a woman so amazing as that?" Catherine asked softly, her eyes full of love for him.

"And that's it? Just accept it all and fall neatly in line with what destiny wants for us?" Dylan asked, stubborn to the end.

"It's not what destiny wants," Catherine said. "Don't

you see? It's what you want. You're here, aren't you? You've left your woman behind, devastated. And from the sounds of it, I doubt she'll be waiting around for you to come back, so again, I'll reiterate my assessment of your intelligence. But nobody is telling you what to do, Dylan. Only you can listen to your heart and trust what you want. So what is it?"

"I want to be with her," Dylan said automatically, surprised to realize it was completely and inexplicably true.

"Then why did you leave her behind?" Catherine asked.

"I… aww, shite. Because I'm an idiot," Dylan said, raking his hand through his hair.

"I hope you know how to grovel, because I suspect this beautiful pirate queen of yours will take no prisoners," Catherine called after him, but Dylan was already racing to his car, the panic of what he might be losing etched on his face.

Catherine looked down at the fat cat who brushed against her leg.

"I think that went well, don't you?"

In response, the cat bit a flower and Catherine narrowed her eyes at him.

"I see someone doesn't want dinner."

CHAPTER 42

"This has been the best gift ever," Fi said as they sipped a mimosa, the sparkling blue waters of the Mediterranean shimmering before them.

After Dylan had left, Grace had needed an out. At first, she'd briefly considered going to find the cottage where her dreams had been shattered. But that seemed too self-indulgent, or perhaps morose, so instead she'd caved to Fi's demands that she visit her in Italy. Rosie had happily gone off with Margaret and Sean, who were staying for a week at Keelin and Flynn's house just over from the cottage. Her work for New York was currently at a stand-still, as the products had all been shipped. With nothing to do but mope, Grace couldn't refuse Fi's offer of a holiday.

It had been exactly what she'd needed.

Grace and Fi had spent the week having a proper girls' holiday, with boat rides on the water and afternoons spent laughing with charming Italian men who were born to flirt. Grace had shopped in all the little boutiques, picking up anything her heart desired, from pretty dangly azure earrings to a deliciously soft leather purse. And a pair of shoes or two. It would be a crime to go to Italy and not buy some shoes, Grace had reasoned, running her hand over the butter-soft leather of her new boots.

Fi had done her best to hook Grace up with every handsome man who crossed her path, but Grace wasn't feeling it. Finally, they had a day of just lounging by the water, and Fi had decided enough was enough.

"You really love him, don't you?" Fi asked, peering at her through polka-dot sunglasses. They were stretched on sun chaises – it was still a little chilly in the season, but warmer than in Ireland. The garden was charming, with climbing vines, a low stone wall, and a breathtaking view of the water. So long as Grace could see the water, she was soothed.

"Aye, I do."

"I thought so. I kind of did a thing. I didn't mean to. Mum yells at me to be better about it," Fi said, nervously drumming her fingers on her leg. Grace glared at her pixie of a friend.

"What did you do?"

"I kind of peeked in your thoughts. I knew how much you loved him. But I had to be sure," Fi said.

"Why did you have to be sure, Fi? Couldn't I have told you in my own time? You know how I feel about that. I try to be good with you," Grace grumbled. Though she couldn't fully read minds, Grace could pick up on flashes here and there, but she always tried to be respectful of her friends.

"I know. It's just that... I've never seen you this distraught. I know you've been putting on a front for me, trying to have fun. But I can tell you just want to be home. With him," Fi said.

"I do. But that really isn't an option for me, Fi. You know that. Hence the whole heartbreak thing," Grace said, sipping on her drink and staring out at the water. "It's just going to take some time for me to get my feet under me and move on."

"Or, you know, you don't have to move on," Fi suggested.

"You want me to go back to him?" Grace said, turning to look at Fi in surprise.

"I think that true love deserves a fighting chance," Fi said evenly.

"I can't fight with someone who walked out," Grace pointed out.

"Yeah, about that," Fi said, a flush creeping up her pretty features.

"What did you do?" Grace asked, rolling to sit up and glare at her friend.

"Well, you know how you told me to take your phone away?" Fi said and Grace felt her stomach go sick.

"You didn't text him, Fi. That would be unforgiveable," Grace hissed, feeling betrayed by her friend.

"Just listen… He called. And called. And called. And messaged. Repeatedly. So, finally I did a thing," Fi shrugged, not looking as guilty as Grace thought she probably should.

"What did you do?" Grace bit out, doing her best to keep her temper in check around her best friend.

"Hello, Grace."

CHAPTER 43

*A*t the sound of Dylan's voice, Grace sprang up and tried to run from the patio, but there was nowhere to go but over the cliffside and down into the sea. Furious with Fi, and unprepared to speak to Dylan, she stared out at the sea and willed herself to breathe.

One breath at a time.

When she finally turned, Fi had made herself scarce. Smart woman, Grace thought as she detailed all the ways she would make her friend suffer.

Her first thought, when she could finally bring herself to look at Dylan, was that he looked tired. And like he'd lost a little weight. Not that she cared, Grace reminded herself as she crossed her arms over her chest.

"I came back to the cottage. The next day," Dylan said, his voice hoarse with emotion. "But you were already gone."

"So? Did you think I'd be there to greet you with open arms?" Grace shrugged and looked away, so frustrated with herself for wanting to run to him and hug him.

"No, I didn't expect that. I didn't expect you to be a coward, though," Dylan said and Grace looked back at him, anger flashing through her.

"Coward? I'm not the one who walked," Grace said, moving forward to poke her finger into his chest. "I'm not the one who wasn't strong enough to stand for us. To give us a chance."

"I know, Grace. I'm the coward. I couldn't see what you saw. But know that I just needed some time to process," Dylan said, his face miserable. "You've had ages to come to terms with magick, with destiny, with crazy dreams and past lives. I've had days. I know I screwed up, but can you cut me some slack? It's a hell of a lot to process on the fly, let alone when you want to change your whole life for someone."

"Change your whole life? What are you changing? Oh... the cultural center? I'm so sorry that you have to move it," Grace griped at him. "I didn't say you couldn't build it. It's not the end of the world to switch locations."

"That's not what I'm talking about," Dylan said, and pulled a package out of the messenger bag he wore. He held it out to her until she took it, looking warily from him to the folder.

"What is this?"

"Open it and see," Dylan suggested.

Grace opened it and scanned the contents, her heart blooming with hope as she realized what he'd done.

"You've done the right thing," Grace said, her voice cracking.

"Aye, the land is yours. I've signed it over to you. You're right. It should stay in your family," Dylan said.

"That's… that's incredibly kind of you," Grace said, straightening her back, "And the right thing to do. I commend you for that."

"Except I'll be needing you to sign off on Clause Number 39," Dylan said, nodding to the file.

"Clause… what? I'm sure this can be worked out another time," Grace grumbled, frustrated and flustered at the prospect of having to read paperwork when the man she loved was throwing her emotions into a tailspin.

"No, it really can't. I'll need you to make a decision on that now," Dylan said, his face set in hard lines. Annoyed, Grace bent her head to the paperwork and flipped through the pages until she found Clause Number 39.

"This long lease of land is transferred into the name of Ms. Grace O'Brien if she accepts the irrevocable right of a tenant to share the cottage located at Grace's Cove," Grace read, then whipped her head at up and glared at him. "A tenant? I don't think so."

"Read on," Dylan suggested.

"The tenancy is solely granted to one Mr. Dylan Kelly…" Grace's voice caught and she looked up from the paperwork, her mouth dropping open to find Dylan kneeling before her.

"What… what does this mean?" Grace gasped.

"And here I'm being called the dumb one all the time," Dylan teased, and then looked up at her, his heart in his eyes. "Before you decide on accepting the clause, I have something else for you."

Grace took the package he offered, which was much heavier than she expected from a man kneeling on the ground. Tucking the paperwork beneath her arm, she hastily unwrapped the paper from the package. When she saw what it was, tears flowed freely.

My heart for yours.

"You found the cottage," Grace whispered, holding the chunk of stone they'd so painstakingly engraved all those years before.

"I found the cottage. And brought this to you to show you that I believe you, I believe in our love, and I was a fool to turn my back on it just because I didn't understand or accept it yet. Will you accept me, Grace, my love? For all my faults and failings, will you take me as your lover, your husband, your love of all time? I'd be lost without you – I didn't realize that I'm nothing without you until I met you once again in this lifetime. Now the pieces all fit together and I know with every fiber of my being that you're the one for me."

Dylan held up yet another package, causing Grace to laugh and cry at the same time. She put the papers down, then lay the stone engraving on top of them, before accepting the box from him. When she opened it, Grace's heart soared.

"It looks like the cove," Grace whispered, meeting Dylan's eyes. The ring, a brilliant blue sapphire with a perfect half-circle of diamonds set in a gold band, shimmered with life and love.

"So?" Dylan asked, hope in his eyes, "Will you accept Clause Number 39? It's irrevocable, you know."

"Aye, I do. Faults, stubbornness, and big heart and all," Grace laughed, leaping into his arms.

"We're forever bound, once more. My heart for yours…" Dylan whispered against her lips.

"Through all time," Grace agreed.

EPILOGUE

"So you're telling me you haven't spilled a word of it?" Dylan asked, laughing as Grace dragged him down the street to the pub. It was a busy Saturday night a few days later, as they'd had trouble leaving a delighted Fi, who was already planning their wedding.

"I haven't. And since Fi's sworn to secrecy, it will be a surprise to all," Grace said. She had only called ahead to let people know they would be back in town. They'd missed the second town meeting, but from the number of emails, phone calls, and text messages that had poured through both their phones, it was apparent that the village had agreed unanimously to approve the design and vision of the cultural center. To the surprise of all, Mr. Murphy had donated his house, which was located close to the harbor with a large yard and small outbuilding, for the center. He was pleased as punch to make something useful out of his childhood home, and Liam had sent an email explaining that it truly was the perfect spot for the center.

"If only we'd come to that conclusion before we'd

gone through all the drama and headaches," Grace had griped, but Dylan had only laughed and pulled her back to bed.

"Then I wouldn't have known what a headstrong and perfect match you are for me, my love," Dylan said, kissing her breathless.

"From where I'm sitting, I'd be saying you're the stubborn one," Grace said, and laughed when he poked her in the ribs.

"We owe Mr. Murphy a drink," Dylan decided, pulling the door open to a packed pub. Word had gotten out that they were back in town and everyone in the village wanted to see who was left standing after their battle for the ages.

Silence filled the room as all eyes turned to look at them, even the musicians playing a jaunty tune in the booth sliding the song to an abrupt stop.

"Well? Did you two figure things out then?" Cait asked, her hands on her hips.

"Aye, that we did," Grace said and held up her hand to show the ring, which sparkled in the pub lights. A cheer went up and in seconds they were swarmed with well-wishers, both Grace and Dylan being roundly kissed and hugged.

"Wait, we have something to settle," Liam called to Cait, and the pub went quiet again.

"I'm already on it, can't you see, Liam?" Cait grumbled, flipping through a fat leatherbound book she'd pulled on to the bar. Pushing her hair from her eyes, she narrowed a look at Dylan.

"What day did you propose, young man?"

"Three days ago, now," Dylan said.

Cait nodded and flipped through the pages, scanning her notes.

"And the winner of the bet on what day they'd get their heads out of their arses and fall for each other..." Cait smiled.

"You bet on us?" Grace said, hands on hips as she surveyed the crowd in outrage.

"Of course we did. You're just mad you weren't in on it," Cait said.

"Who's the winner, Cait?"

"That'd be our fine Mr. Murphy – the hero in this story, it seems," Cait beamed. Mr. Murphy clapped, so delighted was he that he almost toppled off his little bar stool. "To the tune of one thousand thirty-nine euros."

"Drinks on me!" Mr. Murphy cried, and the pub cheered in delight.

"Now, how could I not expect this in a town named after you?" Dylan laughed against her ear and Grace leaned into him, delighted to be back in his arms again, across all these centuries.

Fiona smiled from where she stood behind Cait, always a presence in their lives, content to see her family happy and well-cared for. Turning, she slipped into John's waiting arms.

"A love for all times... much like ours, my pretty Fiona."

"Aye, John, it is at that. My heart for yours."

AFTERWORD

Ireland holds a special place in my heart – a land of dreamers and for dreamers. There's nothing quite like cozying up next to a fire in a pub and listening to a session or having a cup of tea while the rain mists outside the window. I'll forever be enchanted by her rocky shores and I hope you enjoy this series as much as I enjoyed writing it. Thank you for taking part in my world, I hope that my stories bring you great joy.

Have you read books from my other series? Join our little community by signing up for my newsletter for updates on island-living, fun giveaways, and how to follow me on social media!
http://eepurl.com/1LAiz.

or at my website
www.triciaomalley.com

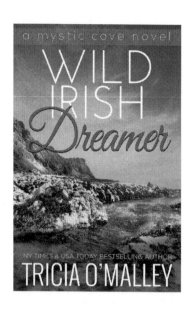

Available now as an e-book, paperback or audiobook!!!

Available from Amazon

* * *

The following is an excerpt from
Wild Irish Dreamer
Book 8 in the Mystic Cove Series

CHAPTER 1

You almost lost him.

Fi awoke in a sweaty mess of sheets, her heart hammering in her chest, her mind stuck in the boggy ground between waking and sleep. Having shot upright at the voice that raged in her dream, she now plopped back to her pillows, gasping, and attempted to sift through the images that threatened to slip from her mind. It was the cove, she was sure of that, for no dreams ever spoke to her as vividly as the ones that came from the enchanted waters in the cove. The problem was, this wasn't her first time – and likely not her last – having prophetic dreams involving her hometown.

It was her bloodline that had enchanted the waters there, after all.

It was probably just another dumb tourist who refused to listen to the advice of the locals. Fi sighed and rubbed a hand over her face, willing her breathing to calm down. Every year, someone was seriously injured at the cove. Despite the posted warnings, despite the local people educating visitors about the vicious undertow, someone always insisted on trying to venture down the steep trail to the deceptively tranquil beach in the cove. They quickly learned their mistake, they *always* did, but sometimes at a steep price.

The cove was magickal, as was her blood, a gift which Fi often did her best to suppress. It wasn't that she detested what had been passed down to her through her bloodline – it was more that Fi just wanted to do everything on her own. She'd been like that since she came screaming from her mother's womb, ready to take on the world, and nobody could tell her differently. Sometimes the gifts of magick that had been passed down from the great Grace O'Malley herself came in useful for Fi, but for the most part, she tried to ignore them; it was vitally important to her that she conquer the world without any extra help.

The dreams, though – those were another story.

"Who am I losing?" Fi demanded out loud, closing her eyes and willing herself to see. Of course, the one time she *did* want her gifts to work, all she could get was vague snatches of the cove and someone in incredible pain. Worried it could be someone close, Fi checked the time and picked up her phone.

"Aye, and to what do I owe this pleasure? Me own wayward daughter, running about the world with not a moment to call her mum."

Fi grinned at Cait's words through the phone, having just spoken with her two days ago.

"I'm positively a stranger these days, I am. 'Tis a right shame I bring to the family," Fi agreed.

"Your father is convinced you've become a groupie to a band and have gone to drugs now."

"A groupie? That's insulting. I'd start me own band, that's the truth of it," Fi scoffed, offended that her father would think she'd just blindly follow some deadbeat musicians around the world.

"Ah, so it's just the drugs then," Cait said.

"Naturally. But I just sell them. It's how I fund this fancy lifestyle of mine. But I don't use. Never get high on your own supply, as they say," Fi said, stretching her legs out and letting her mum's voice soothe her pounding heart.

"'Tis the smartest way. It's why I've only a nip or two of the whiskey when I'm working," Cait agreed.

"Is… everything okay?" Fi asked, closing her eyes so she could read her mother's voice.

"I believe it to be. Have you had a dream then?"

"Aye, about the cove. Maybe have someone give it a check and make sure another tourist hasn't ended up down there?"

"Shane, your daughter says check the cove. Have a call over there, will ye?"

"Tell her to come home."

"She'll come when she's ready."

"Tell him I'll be home for Grace's hen party soon," Fi promised.

"Oh, right. Have you ideas for it then?"

"I do…"

Fi spent the next half hour chatting comfortably with her mum while the anxiety drifted from her neck and shoulders. All seemed to be well at the cove, so Fi shrugged it off as an odd dream and left it at that. No need to search for more troubles – she already had enough on her plate. Speaking of which, she needed to finish her project for today so she could spend the rest of the day shopping for supplies for Grace's party. But first, coffee.

In the time since she'd been living on the Amalfi Coast, Fi had learned to love strong coffee like her Italian neighbors, though she preferred to linger over it on her small terrace overlooking the water if the weather was nice instead of taking it like a shot at the counter of the coffee shop below. Try as she might, Fi had never mastered the art of waking quickly, and she'd learned to build time into her mornings to ease into the day and wake her brain up. Fi now took this routine to sit by her window where she could read the paper – yes, the actual paper – and savor her morning espresso.

As a translator specializing in Italian, Spanish, and French, Fi thought it necessary to immerse herself where she worked. Hence the Italian paper, which she read every morning, front to back. It helped to loosen her mind and get her thinking in Italian, after which she could sit down to whatever contract she was translating and work with confidence.

Today, though, her brain struggled to focus. Inexplicably, she was drawn back to the memory of a man whose image periodically drifted through her mind. Liam Mulder. She wondered where he was these days.

She hadn't been long out of university when she'd first met him. Fi thought back, closing her eyes and tipping her face up to the sun that struggled to shine through the clouds.

She'd been green, eager for work, and ready to take on

the world. Sean Burke, Margaret's husband and kin to Fi, had hired her to translate a contract for his shipping company up in Dublin. Fi still remembered her first day: Dressed in a smart black suit and wearing sky-high red heels, she'd walked into the meeting and realized just how egregiously overdressed she was. Scattered around the table were a slew of men in denim pants and button-down shirts, sleeves casually rolled to their elbows. Immediately recognizing her dismay, Sean had welcomed her and put her at ease, a warning look in his eyes for the others. Only Liam had smiled widely at her, including her in on the joke she'd made of herself. She'd immediately taken to him.

Through their negotiations – Sean was acquiring two new ships from an Italian shipping company – Fi had found herself laughing and chatting with Liam. There was something about the careless confidence he'd exuded that had pulled Fi in.

When he'd invited her for a drink after work, Fi had eagerly accepted. But when she arrived back at Sean's house, where she'd been staying the night to catch up with him and Margaret, he had called to cancel.

"Work conflicts," Liam had said, apologizing gracefully.

"It's not our time," Fi had replied, then pulled the phone away to look at it in shock. Where had that come from?

"Is that so? Well, you'll have to let me know when it is," Liam had said, and Fi had hung up, her cheeks flushed with embarrassment. What was wrong with her?

"That Liam?" Sean had asked, watching her carefully from across the table.

"Aye, that was. He called off meeting up tonight." Fi shrugged.

"That's a lad. Wouldn't want to mix business and pleasure," Sean had said, and then gruffly changed the subject. That was when Fi had realized Sean had scared Liam off.

Goddess save her from overbearing family. Vowing then and there to follow her dream of being independent and traveling the world, Fi had eagerly accepted the next client project that allowed her to travel. Off she'd gone, and Liam had faded into the past.

Just a memory… or so she'd thought.

THE ISLE OF DESTINY SERIES

ALSO BY TRICIA O'MALLEY

Stone Song

Sword Song

Spear Song

Sphere Song

* * *

A completed series.

Available in audio, e-book & paperback!

"Love this series. I will read this multiple times. Keeps you on the edge of your seat. It has action, excitement and romance all in one series."

- Amazon Review

THE WILDSONG SERIES

ALSO BY TRICIA O'MALLEY

Song of the Fae

Melody of Flame

Chorus of Ashes

* * *

"The magic of Fae is so believable. I read these books in one sitting and can't wait for the next one. These are books you will reread many times."

- Amazon Review

Available in audio, e-book & paperback!

Available Now

THE SIREN ISLAND SERIES

ALSO BY TRICIA O'MALLEY

Good Girl

Up to No Good

A Good Chance

Good Moon Rising

Too Good to Be True

A Good Soul

In Good Time

* * *

A completed series.

Available in audio, e-book & paperback!

"Love her books and was excited for a totally new and different one! Once again, she did NOT disappoint! Magical in multiple ways and on multiple levels. Her writing style, while similar to that of Nora Roberts, kicks it up a notch!! I want to visit that island, stay in the B&B and meet the gals who run it! The characters are THAT real!!!" - Amazon Review

THE ALTHEA ROSE SERIES

ALSO BY TRICIA O'MALLEY

One Tequila

Tequila for Two

Tequila Will Kill Ya (Novella)

Three Tequilas

Tequila Shots & Valentine Knots (Novella)

Tequila Four

A Fifth of Tequila

A Sixer of Tequila

Seven Deadly Tequilas

Eight Ways to Tequila

Tequila for Christmas (Novella)

"Not my usual genre but couldn't resist the Florida Keys setting. I was hooked from the first page. A fun read with just the right amount of crazy! Will definitely follow this series."- Amazon Review

A completed series.

Available in audio, e-book & paperback!

THE MYSTIC COVE SERIES

Wild Irish Heart

Wild Irish Eyes

Wild Irish Soul

Wild Irish Rebel

Wild Irish Roots: Margaret & Sean

Wild Irish Witch

Wild Irish Grace

Wild Irish Dreamer

Wild Irish Christmas (Novella)

Wild Irish Sage

Wild Irish Renegade

Wild Irish Moon

* * *

"I have read thousands of books and a fair percentage have been romances. Until I read Wild Irish Heart, I never had a book actually make me believe in love."- Amazon Review

A completed series.

Available in audio, e-book & paperback!

CONTACT ME

I hope my books have added a little magick into your life. If you have a moment to add some to my day, you can help by telling your friends and leaving a review. Word-of-mouth is the most powerful way to share my stories. Thank you.

Love books? What about fun giveaways? Nope? Okay, can I entice you with underwater photos and cute dogs? Let's stay friends, receive my emails and contact me by signing up at my website

www.triciaomalley.com

Or find me on Facebook and Instagram.
@triciaomalleyauthor

AUTHOR'S ACKNOWLEDGEMENT

First, and foremost, I'd like to thank my family and friends for their constant support, advice, and ideas. You've all proven to make a difference on my path. And, to my beta readers, I love you for all of your support and fascinating feedback!

And last, but never least, my two constant companions as I struggle through words on my computer each day - Briggs and Blue.